UNREVEALED

Cindy L. Freeman

HighTide
Publications, Inc.

Deltaville, Virginia

High Tide Publications, Inc.
1000 Bland Point
Deltaville, Virginia 23043
www.hightidepublications.com

Quantity sales. Special discounts are available on quantity purchases by corporations, associations, and others. For details, contact the "Special Sales Department" at the address above.

Unrevealed, 1st ed.
Edited by Narielle Living (NarielleLiving.com)

Cindy L. Freeman/Unrevealed (http://www.cindylfreeman.com)

ISBN 978-0692548516

A secret is not something unrevealed, but something told privately, in a whisper.

Marcel Pagnol

ACKNOWLEDGMENTS

With an abundance of good literature inundating libraries and bookstores, plus myriad online offerings, what could propel an amateur writer like me to join such a competitive market? I am nearing the end of an entirely different career as a music educator, after all—a satisfying one, too. My answer is simple. A writer must write.

It will take many years to become a *good* writer. I have much to learn. But the people who are generous enough to share their expertise are patiently helping me reach my goal.

I have stories to tell, but every published author knows the story is just the beginning. To successfully express what is on my mind and in my heart, I must revisit the basics of grammar, syntax, Point of View, tense, punctuation, and so much more. I must learn how to find editors and publishers who think my writing will sell. After spending a year or more penning a novel, I must set aside ego and prepare for cuts, rewrites, and rejections. Once a work is published, I must find an audience, then market and sell my books . . . lots of them if I hope to turn a profit.

For supporting every effort along this new journey, I thank Carl Freeman, my steadfast, supportive husband of forty-plus years, who, I think, must grow weary of asking, "Have you reached a stopping point? May I interrupt briefly to tell you that . . . dinner is ready?" Or "the house is on fire?"

Then there is Dr. Beverly Peterson, my first reader, literary adviser and very gentle critic. She embraces my characters and believes in my stories. Whenever the nagging doubts creep in, she encourages me to keep writing. Thanks, Bev, for your unwavering faith.

I am infinitely grateful to Jeanne and Carl Johansen of High Tide Publications for taking a chance on this novice writer and to Narielle Living, my amazing editor at High Tide, for patiently and honestly sharing her mastery of the written word.

Finally, for helping aspiring authors like me promote their published works, I thank Greg Lilly. As a writer and publisher, himself, he understands the challenges of breaking into a rapidly changing industry.

I will keep writing because I must. If I find an appreciative audience, so much the better.

CHAPTER ONE

Howling wind caused every crevice of the old stone mansion to shudder and groan. Beyond the walls of Wellington Manor, driving rain slammed against the window panes like wet towels slapping on a clothesline, but Allison barely noticed. Curled up in the same wingback chair that had wrapped her in comfort more than once during childhood, the young woman embraced a familiar needlepoint pillow. A blazing fire roared in the mammoth fireplace before her. It had taken some effort for Clarence, the caretaker, to bring the ashy beast to life, but now the warmth of crackling logs hugged Allison, dispelling the chill of a late autumn evening.

Mesmerized by hypnotic flames pirouetting before her, Allison's thoughts floated back to memories of a carefree childhood—carefree, that is, until one day when life as she knew it would have taken a vastly different direction had it not been for dutiful measures to protect her from the family's secret.

Thanks to her father's intentional mentoring, Allison had grown into a strong, independent business woman, capable of effective leadership. In the workplace, she made decisions with confidence and adeptly tackled the most challenging issues. Yet, she was often perceived as too young and inexperienced to head an international conglomerate. During working hours, she wore her long, auburn hair in an up-do, dressing in solid, tailored pantsuits to appear authoritative. High heeled pumps, though not a comfortable choice of footwear for her typically long days, added height to her five-foot-four stature, contributing to the air of confidence with which she carried herself. At work, she was all-business; a strict, but fair supervisor, hyper-organized and meticulous. But, no matter how grown up the twenty-seven-year-old executive felt in her father's Madison Avenue high rise, upon crossing the threshold of the family's Long Island estate, she became Allie-the-child, the only heir of Marcus III and Evelyn Harmon.

Three hours earlier she stood at the grave of her beloved father, the recently retired president of Harmon & Harmon Enterprises. Under a sea of black umbrellas, hundreds of mourners gathered to pay their respects. It was no surprise to find the church filled to overflowing, but given the ominous weather forecast, Allison hardly expected so many of them to attend the graveside service.

Only a few days ago she had spoken to Daddy on the phone, his voice sounding as robust as ever, the conversation concluding with his usual, "I love you, Allie Cat." She couldn't recall exactly when the nickname, Kitten, had changed to Allie Cat, but both monikers had always made her feel loved and special. Not that the wealthy heiress had ever been overindulged, but Allison knew she was adored by the affluent and highly regarded Marcus Harmon. *How could he be gone?* She wondered, tears of grief dotting the pillow on her lap. *He hadn't even been sick!* He had rarely been sick. He was supposed to be enjoying his golden years, playing golf, traveling to exotic destinations, and finally finding time to read the hundreds of volumes in his library with the walnut paneling and comfortable leather chairs. Collecting first editions had been one of Marcus's few hobbies, but a busy career prevented him from actually reading more than a handful of them.

Marcus would not permit any child of his to grow up with a sense of entitlement. Oh, no! His children would learn, at an early age—just as he had—that with privilege came responsibility. Having watched his own father, the son of German immigrants, train at the knee of his father before him, Marcus had quickly learned there are no free rides in life, not even in the country of boundless opportunity. Wealth, prestige, and privilege must be earned through hard work and sacrifice. Both a strong work ethic and the textile industry that his grandfather had built from a small upholstery business would be passed on to his heir, Marcus Gregory Harmon IV.

In the absence of a son, Marcus's attention and careful grooming focused on Allison, whose mother, Evelyn, had died of pancreatic cancer when her daughter was only six years old. Many of Allison's childhood memories remained fuzzy, flashing briefly through her mind like sparks from the perfectly cured wood crackling before her tonight, but lately they had grown increasingly vivid. Often, she found herself distracted at work and jarringly awakened at night.

CHAPTER 2

Allison never questioned the notion that she would one day take control of H & H Enterprises. Her entire life had revolved around that momentous, yet routine, day two years ago when the torch passed seamlessly from father to daughter. Marcus's carefully orchestrated plan of succession began in earnest when Allison was a mere eight years old. At every opportunity, she would accompany him to work, not only during summer vacations, but also on every school holiday and most Saturdays. This habit continued throughout high school, leaving little time for social pursuits, but Allison didn't need a social life, or so she rationalized at the time. She never questioned the master plan which led to a business degree from Columbia followed by an MBA. During her university years, she could live at home and still be involved at H & H. Well before Marcus retired, she had learned the textile industry inside and out. Most of the actual work was done overseas now, and by the time she turned twenty-one, Allison had traveled to five countries and studied the most intricate detail of every operation.

Marcus had always been patient with his daughter's questions, even welcoming the opportunity to explain yet another aspect of the business. Often father and daughter would sit in that very room, drinking wine from Marcus's well-stocked cellar and rehashing the day's events. He would listen attentively to Allison's ideas and help her sort out the pros and cons of many a proposal. She was the one who convinced her father to shut down the cashmere factory in China and refuse to renew the contract until assured that the weavers would receive a fair wage. At the risk of losing a four-million-dollar contract, Allison—only nineteen at the time—and the vice president in charge of overseas marketing had flown to Hefei and successfully negotiated an acceptable agreement with Xiao Zhèng. Whom would she question now? To whom would she go for advice and guidance?

More than once, Allison's grandfather had tried to convince his son that women had no place in the business world. "They just don't have a head for it," he would say. But, before his passing in 1999, the elder Harmon had given his blessing to the plan of succession. It would place his granddaughter at the helm of the company that he and his father before him had invested a lifetime building. Harmon & Harmon had expanded and flourished even through wartime and depression years because of shrewd business practices and personal sacrifices.

Now Allison was alone—an orphan in her childhood home and CEO of a billion-dollar conglomerate. Overwhelmed and grief-stricken, she gave in to the flow of tears that she held at bay all day. As the storm continued to rage outside, lights flickered throughout the manor and finally extinguished. But amid the leaping flames in the hearth and disturbing flashes of memory, Allison barely noticed the darkness. Once again she struggled to make sense of strange, jumbled fragments…

Oma and Opa are talking to Daddy in hushed tones…

Mommy is crying. Daddy's voice: "…too late, Evie…try to forget."

Then another image flashed through her mind.

Two men arguing behind the closed doors of Daddy's study:

"…can't continue…deserves to know…"

"Don't be a fool!"

Once again, her confused mind somersaulted back to the present moment, and Allison was left frustrated that she could neither make sense of the fragmented thoughts nor dismiss them for good.

Decisions must be made, decisions Allison had assumed would not require her attention for years to come. Marcus was only sixty-nine. By today's standards, he still had many years left to enjoy the fruits of his labor. To his daughter, he had always seemed invincible. "Massive heart attack," the doctor had pronounced. After that, frequent nightmares began to plague Allison's sleep.

A child—or is it an animal?—is locked in a room. Whimpering sounds come from behind the door. There is a sense that rescuing this pitiful creature is her responsibility and hers alone. Someone hands her a key, but either it doesn't fit the lock or she drops it and can't find it in the dark. Desperate to get to the source of the distressing cries, she always fails. Invariably she awakens apprehensive and defeated.

Word about her father's death would travel quickly and Allison would have to be ready first thing Monday morning with a statement about the future of H & H. Although she had functioned as Chief Executive Officer for the past two years, her father retained ownership of the company. As she assumed the presidency, she would need to reassure employees and clients, worldwide, that business would proceed as usual. She would have to face meetings with corporate lawyers, department heads, stockholders, and of course, the press. Someone—she didn't even know who—had managed to keep reporters at bay during the funeral proceedings, but that wouldn't last long. There would be a flurry of questions to answer and stacks of papers to review and sign. In addition, her father's personal estate had to be addressed and a reading of his will scheduled.

What would she do with the manor? She hadn't lived here in several years, not since purchasing her condo in the city. While she loved this monstrosity of a house with its old world grandeur and neatly manicured grounds, it would surely become a liability now. Yet, it broke her heart to think of abandoning her beloved childhood home forever and dismissing its loyal staff. Martha, the housekeeper, had been with the family since before Allison was born. Felix, her father's driver, arrived some four or five years later and Clarence, while not as longstanding as the others, had become equally as faithful an employee. Even Gretchen, whom Daddy had recently hired to help Martha, was working out splendidly.

Amid Allison's forlorn reverie, Martha entered the room carrying a lighted candle. "Miss Allison," she inquired quietly, tenderly. "Will you take dinner in the dining room? Or I could prepare a tray, if you prefer." As she emerged from the shadows into the glow of the fire, Allison observed, for the first time, how much Martha had aged. It occurred to her that she had no idea how old this woman was. She had always been there, a part of Allison's life for as long as she can remember—a part of the Harmon family since well before her birth. She knew that Martha once had a family of her own, that her husband and only son were killed in an automobile accident many years ago. She remembered when Martha moved into the manor, taking a suite in the original servants' quarters.

"I'm not very hungry," Allison replied. "Just leave a tray. Maybe I'll eat something later."

"Yes, Miss." Martha turned to go, hesitated, and circled back to face her mistress again.

"Miss Allison, I wanted to say how sorry I am about your father. We'll all miss him."

"Thank you, Martha. I can't believe he's gone."

"Miss Allison, I…" Allison glanced up from the mesmerizing flames to observe a strangely unnerving expression on the old woman's face. But then it was gone.

"Martha, what is it?"

"Nothing, Miss. I'll have Gretchen bring your tray," she said, fading into the darkness.

CHAPTER 3

Will I ever finish school and get on with my life? Jack Sanderling wondered. As much as he enjoyed studying at the Academy of Fine Arts in Manhattan, he had not intended to become a career-student. After four years of college and three years of graduate school, he was eager to move on to his chosen profession. Living in New York City had been a venturesome undertaking for a young man from rural Virginia. He longed to return to his beautiful mountains and the slower pace of life there, at least for a visit. Of course, he would never be able to pursue his career in the tiny town of Bedford—population: 6,000—but he could use a hometown "fix" and some of his mother's heavenly cooking. Once Jack finished and defended his doctoral dissertation, the end would finally be in sight, and he could start circulating his resume. Surely the fellowship to study in Paris, when added to his already impressive list of accomplishments, would facilitate his lifelong goal—securing a position as head curator at a major museum.

Jack experienced no shortage of female attention since settling in Manhattan. After all, women have always been attracted to tall, dark haired, handsome men. Standing six feet tall and muscular in build, he turned women's heads on a daily basis. The problem with encouraging overtures, though, is that women insist upon building relationships, and relationships require both time and energy. Jack simply didn't have enough of either to commit to a serious romance, not yet, anyway. First, he had to finish his interminable education and then land the job of his dreams.

Organized sports never interested Jack, but despite a demanding academic schedule, he managed to stay in shape by running and working out almost daily. Central Park was his favorite place to run. The rocky mounds dotting the park were slightly reminiscent of his beloved Blue Ridge, and the mid-Manhattan oasis never failed to deliver much needed respite from the hustle and bustle of city life.

Initially, Jack thought he wanted to become a professional artist, an aspiration which came as no surprise to his mother, Silvia. After all, his paternal grandfather was the famous Virginian artist, John Sanderling, for whom both Jack and his father were named; and before his father died when Jack and his brother, Simon, were only four and two, respectively, John Sanderling II had worked as a graphic artist for an advertising agency in Roanoke.

Jack began sketching at an early age. As soon as he could hold a pencil, the boy filled notebook after notebook with drawings of airplanes, animals, race cars, flowers, clouds, anything and everything. In elementary school, young Jack would draw in the margins of his textbooks and fill his composition books with doodles. Almost from birth, it seemed, the child was intrigued by shape, form, and perspective. On more than one occasion during his elementary school years, he would be sent to his mother's classroom just down the hall to spend an hour or so with a giant pink eraser.

The best birthday present Jack ever received was his very own easel. He was ten years old at the time. Along with canvases of varying sizes came a supply of colored pencils, charcoal chalk, and water colors, also an array of brushes and a wooden painter's palette. Then, after his fifth grade field trip to the art museum in Lynchburg, Jack was unequivocally hooked on art. In seventh grade art class, he was introduced to oil paints. The way he could swirl the brush across the canvas to create texture was positively captivating. The young artist discovered that by mixing just the right amount of blue and green and adding a drop or two of red, he could recreate the exact color of his beloved Blue Ridge Mountains at sunset. He marveled at how many different shades of green could be formulated by adding a bit of black here or a dab of white there.

It hadn't been easy for Silvia Sanderling to raise two active, strong-willed boys by herself, but somehow she managed by sheer grit and determination. Quite intentionally, she surrounded her sons with positive male role models while encircling herself with many supportive friends. Everyone in Bedford knew everyone else, it seemed, and everyone in the Sanderling family's inner circle attended the same United Methodist church. In Bedford, if you didn't belong to one of some twenty Baptist churches, you were a United Methodist. Both her active church life and her fervent faith gave Silvia the strength to carry on after her husband's death. Her church also provided a stable pool of honorable men to mentor her growing sons. In order to pay the bills, the young mother was forced to return to full-time teaching, but, fortunately, their grandfather's estate included generous trust funds for the boys' education.

John Sanderling, the artist, had never taken a formal art lesson. His was a natural talent. His namesake also displayed an inherent gift, but Jack found he wanted more from art than just painting and drawing. Besides, he knew he could never live up to the legendary figure that was his grandfather, especially in his hometown. In the town of Bedford, there were only two memorials: one, the national D-Day Memorial, commemorated the inordinate number of fallen soldiers from World War II, and the other celebrated the town's home grown artist, John W. Sanderling.

Jack soon discovered that he hungered to learn everything there was to know about art, becoming especially curious about the evolution of visual arts throughout history. A visit to the Smithsonian museums in Washington, D.C. sealed his fate. Even before entering high school, Jack began searching in earnest for the best art schools in the country. He settled on the New York Academy, not only because of the school's excellent reputation, but because he knew that opportunities for landing a position as a curator would be most prevalent in a major urban setting. First, he would need to complete an undergraduate degree since the Academy only accepted post graduate students. So, he applied and was accepted at NYU.

Each summer since arriving in New York, Jack worked at a different museum in the City, hoping to gain as much experience and exposure as possible. From the Metropolitan to the Guggenheim and everything in between, he accepted whatever job was available. Whether dusting picture frames, unpacking boxes, directing tourists or doing research in the basement archives, he considered it a privilege to spend his days in the presence of some of the world's master painters and sculptors.

CHAPTER 4

For the past six years, Jack shared a studio apartment located a mere two blocks from Times Square with his Jamaican roommate, Zavie Johnson. Finding the place was a stroke of luck. No matter that it required walking up four flights of stairs, or that it boasted not one inch more than 900 square feet of space, or that two of the four windows overlooked an alley where the building's trash dumpsters are kept. For two twenty-something young men from humble backgrounds trying to make it in the Big Apple, it represented a piece of heaven. Jack slept on the sofa and Zavie used the Murphy bed. Every other year, the sleeping arrangements reversed despite Zavie's insistence that he would be perfectly content using the sofa all the time. After sharing a bed with two ever-expanding brothers, a mattress on the floor seemed luxurious to him. But Jack insisted upon alternating the sleeping arrangements.

Adjacent to the sleeping area was a kitchenette where simple meals could be prepared, but other than breakfast, Jack and Zavie ate most meals at the few affordable cafes and fast-food restaurants in the vicinity.

The two young men met nearly seven years earlier in the Admissions Office of NYU—or rather outside the Admissions

Office and hit it off immediately. Since the check-in line extended out the door and down the sidewalk that first day, they had plenty of time to get acquainted. At first, Jack found it difficult to understand Zavie through his heavy accent, especially when he slipped into Patois, but, as Jack listened carefully, he discovered that often the Jamaican's English was more proper than his own, and his clever wit made him most entertaining.

"What brings you so far from home?" Jack asked as the queue inched forward at a snail's pace.

"Well, now, I could ask deh same of you, yes?" Zavie countered, while his eyes held their characteristic twinkle.

"Okay, so Jamaica isn't that much farther away than Virginia," Jack acquiesced, "but at least we get snow where I come from. I hope you know what you're in for when winter comes."

"I have seen pictures of deh snow, and I theenk it will be fun."

"It's fun the first time, but after that, it's just annoying and *cold*."

"We shall see, Mon," Zavie answered, smiling. "Besides, mi have fancy new boots and coat to test and colorful hat that makes Zavie look very handsome. I will be irresistible to deh women, yes?" He struck a model's pose, making Jack laugh. Jack observed that, with Zavie's perfect physique, he could easily make a living modeling for the resident sculptors if he chose. Standing a little taller than Jack, with lanky, muscular limbs, the islander's flawless skin was the closest to actual black Jack had ever seen. Jack learned that Zavie hailed from a small, poor village on the island, and his parents worked at menial jobs in the tourism industry. He had two brothers and three sisters, all younger than he. Zavie explained that his artistic talent was discovered by a wealthy American businessman who had arranged for him to apply for a scholarship. He earned a full ride to study at both NYU and the Academy, including housing.

"I will work hard in school and sell many paintings so mi parents and bruddahs and sistahs can have a big house and no worries. Mi Mum and Dad, they work too hard."

"So does my Mom," added Jack. "She raised my brother and me by herself, and I'm sure we were a handful."

"What happened to your faduh, if you don't mind mi asking?"

"I don't mind. It was a long time ago. He was in the National Guard and his unit got called to the Middle East. It was supposed to be a temporary assignment, just to assist the ground troops for six months or so. He never came back."

"Oh, sorry, Mon," Zavie responded with genuine sympathy. "I don't think mi Mum could manage on her own. Of course, without mi faduh, she wouldn't have six kids to raise, yeh?"

By the time Jack and Zavie reached the front of the line, they had become fast friends who were making arrangements to room together. But after a year of dorm life, the pair was more than ready to live off campus. The challenge would be to find an apartment within walking distance of school and, in New York City, one they could afford. Throughout the summer months prior to their sophomore year they searched in vain, nearly reconciled to spending another year in the dormitory.

Then, one sweltering evening in late August, Jack got a text message from Zavie, with instructions to meet him at a restaurant on the east side. "Don't be late, Dude," it said. "I have big surprise… well, not so big, but bashy!" Zavie tended to slip into Patois whenever he got excited. After a short subway ride from campus,

Jack located the restaurant where Zavie and a real estate broker had already ordered drinks.

"A toast to our new apartment," Zavie exclaimed after introducing Jack to the realtor.

"What are you talking about, Lunatic?" Jack asked, skeptical.

"You'll see. Now drink up, so we can show you."

Moments later the trio stood in front of a classic brick building that seemed strangely out of place, wedged between two modern structures, like a row house that had lost its row; but the architecture had character and, best of all, the building was located only two blocks from Times Square. Surprisingly, a couple of nice shade trees lined the front sidewalk. Once inside, they discovered the building had been converted into studio apartments, each occupying one full level. The foyer had been restored to its original nineteenth century glory, but with modern lighting. As they ascended the stairwell to the fourth floor, the realtor regurgitated his spiel for the second time that day.

"You gentlemen don't realize how fortunate you are to find this place. The previous couple had to break their lease and move suddenly. It's fully furnished and you can move in immediately," said the realtor, whose name Jack had already forgotten. "A small shared laundry facility is in the basement."

"Rhaatid! Can you believe it?" Zavie exclaimed, slapping his friend on the back. "And wait till you see the hardwood floors," he added, excitedly. "You could eat off them. Well, maybe not spaghetti," he clarified, "kind of messy, you know?"

For such a small apartment, it was surprisingly bright and airy. Along the front wall, two narrow windows overlooked the street.

From where the men were standing, only lush, green tree limbs were visible, creating the illusion of a far more suburban setting. Two identical windows overlooked the rear alley and the building beyond, one leading to the fire escape and the other supporting the air conditioning unit. To the left was a charming, exposed brick wall, and nestled in the corner stood a modern kitchenette—emphasis on the "ette"—with a shiny granite countertop and stainless steel appliances. An updated bathroom and relatively generous closet completed the space.

"Wait—where's the bedroom?" Jack asked as he peered into the tiny, gleaming bathroom.

"Ah! Wait 'til you see this," answered Zavie. "Voila!" Pulling on a handle that seemed to disappear into the wall, he revealed a full size Murphy bed.

"You're a natural real estate broker, Mr. Johnson," remarked the realtor. "Let me know if you need a job."

"I have to say, it's absolutely perfect, but can we afford it?" Jack said.

"Dude, it is only 1,995 dollars a month! We can't afford *not* to rent it," answered Zavie. "It's bigger than mi house in Jamaica and so bee-yoo-tee-ful! I can paint palm trees on that wall and it will feel like home. Just kidding," he added quickly before the realtor had time to react.

"We had hoped to live closer to campus, but… the subway ride is only twenty minutes or so," Jack rationalized. "Let's go for it."

CHAPTER 5

The morning after her father's funeral, Allison awakened early in her penthouse condo that overlooked Central Park. She felt like she hadn't slept at all and hoped a brisk walk would clear her still-pounding head. After calling for a security escort, she showered quickly and dressed in her typical workday uniform: solid pantsuit and silk blouse. After an abbreviated application of makeup, she packed her navy heels, a yogurt bar, and a bottle of aspirin in her backpack. Then, donning her Nikes, she grabbed her briefcase, met her escort in the lobby, and struck out for the fifteen-block walk to work. She hoped the usual throng of reporters wouldn't expect her to be out this early.

Allison had never been able to eat breakfast. The thought of food first thing in the morning produced waves of nausea. *I'll stop at one of many Starbucks en route and order a "tall regular" with a shot of espresso,* she decided. The day portended to be long and hectic, offering, thankfully, little opportunity to focus on the sting of sorrow that threatened to consume her.

Allison arrived at H & H a little before seven thirty a.m. Relieved to find the lobby empty, except for the security guard, she hoped that Theo, her trusted assistant, hadn't come in yet. She needed time to gather her thoughts. Typically, Mondays were hectic, but today promised to be overwhelmingly so, especially after a three-day weekend. She rode the elevator to her office, and found that no one was stirring yet in the outer office. She didn't feel ready to face the employees or respond to their well-meaning expressions of condolence just yet. Allison entered her spacious office with its tall windows overlooking 7th Avenue—also known as Fashion Avenue—the office that her father once occupied. The view was unimpressive, but at least she could enjoy the early morning sun filtering through the long sheers, filling the exquisitely appointed room with a cheerful glow. While booting up her computer, Allison changed into her heels and settled in to face a work day that promised to be even more stressful than usual.

Theo, a lanky young man with blond, short-cropped, curly hair arrived at eight-fifteen. He strolled directly into Allison's office, carrying an IPad in one hand and a cup of coffee in the other. He was impeccably dressed, as always.

"Good morning, Ms. Harmon. I thought you might sleep in a little this morning, especially after…"

"Oh, so you decided you could waltz in fifteen minutes late and I wouldn't notice?" she asked with a mock-serious demeanor. She was trying to keep the atmosphere light today and knew Theo would respect her wishes because he respected her. Since day one Theo was consistently prompt and efficient, and Allison clearly expressed, on numerous occasions, how much she appreciated his loyal, competent service both to her and to the firm. Still, they couldn't simply ignore the events of the weekend. Their relationship for the past two years had built trust and honesty—even friendship—between them.

"Ms. Harmon, I just want to say how sorry I am about your father. He was…"

"Thanks, Theo," she interrupted without looking up from the computer. Lifting her eyes to meet his, she added, "Thank you for coming to the service and for the beautiful flowers. I really appreciate everything." There were no tears because she couldn't risk losing control. Tears must be saved for moments of privacy.

"You're welcome. Please let me know if I can do anything to help."

"I will. Thanks. Now, we'd better get started. The stockholders will be here at five p.m., and we need to gather the department heads as soon as possible." Theo sat opposite Allison, placing his coffee cup on the edge of her massive mahogany desk.

"I'll schedule a ten o'clock meeting," he said.

"Perfect. What about Grayson & Grayson? Have they called?"

"Yes, you have a lunch meeting with Zachary Grayson. I ordered sushi."

"Okay, good. Pull up the international time schedule and see if you can coordinate a conference call with the overseas directors. Then, please weed out my inbox. It's overflowing."

"You got it. What about the reporters gathering in the lobby?" Theo asked.

"I must have just missed them," Allison replied, standing. "I knew we couldn't stall them for long, but… have Terri schedule a full press conference for eleven a.m. In the meantime, here's my initial statement. This should stall them temporarily." She pulled a document from the printer and handed it to her assistant.

"Got it. Anything else?" Theo asked, rising to leave.

"Ask Terri to hold any calls that aren't absolutely critical. I need to prepare my board report. Give me thirty minutes; then get Melissa up here so we can go over the financials."

"Done."

CHAPTER 6

"Ladies and gentlemen, I appreciate your attendance at this impromptu meeting." Allison stood at the end of the long conference table, addressing the stockholders. All eyes were focused on her, and, as Allison scanned the room, she noticed that they reflected an air of uncertainty mixed with compassion. Drawing on her father's frequent advice to be proactive, never reactive, the new president of Harmon & Harmon Enterprises was fully prepared to dispel anxiety and answer any questions that might arise.

"First, I want to thank each of you for your expressions of sympathy in the passing of my father. Many of you attended the services and the reception following. I'm very grateful. I know that my father greatly appreciated your commitment to H & H and valued your advice and counsel. I, too, value your service and will continue to rely on your counsel. I assure you the company stands on solid financial ground, and my father has prepared me thoroughly to step into his shoes." Everyone responded with enthusiastic applause.

Feeling slightly embarrassed, but gratified, by the group's show of support, Allison continued. "Thank you," she said. "Although our monthly meeting is scheduled for two weeks from today, I asked Ms.

Donavan to prepare a financial report for this meeting. You'll find a hard copy in your folder." Allison took her seat and relinquished the meeting to Melissa Donovan, CFO, who presented a reassuring report and fielded several questions, primarily in reference to the stock market.

A few additional questions were directed to Allison, but the general atmosphere of the meeting was exactly as she intended to convey: no major changes or surprises were expected. After all, Allison had been running the company for two years with her father as a figurehead. Her assumption of the presidency was a mere formality. But these board members were part owners, as well, and deserved to be kept abreast of every aspect of the operation.

As the meeting drew to a close, Allison announced that the buy-out of a small upholstery business in San Francisco should be finalized before the next meeting and they could expect a full report on the fifteenth. "Thank you, again, for coming. I hope to see all of you then."

Most days, Allison insisted on staying at the office until all loose ends were tied up and her desk was cleared, but tonight she's completely exhausted. More than anything, she needed a relaxing bath and a good night's sleep. Tomorrow morning, she would arrive early, she decided, and dive into that pile of paperwork with renewed energy. As soon as everyone, including Theo, departed, she dialed Felix on her cell phone. He would have the car waiting for her by the time she packed her briefcase, donned her coat, and rode the elevator to the lobby. Back in her office, she noticed the blinking message light on her desk phone. Should she listen or ignore the message? She decided to listen.

It was Martha's voice. "Miss Allison, I just wanted you to know that I sent you some dinner with Felix. I'm sure your first day back has been busy and you won't feel like cooking or going out tonight. You can warm it up in the microwave. Now be sure to eat. You need to keep up your strength." Ever since the death of Allison's mother when Allison was only six, Martha has felt protective of her and responsible for her well-being. "There's so much food here and it'll never get eaten. Please let me know if you'll be coming for dinner, as usual, on Saturday. Okay, bye now."

Allison couldn't help but notice the awkwardness in Martha's voice. Surely, it must feel strange for the woman's employer to be the same little girl that she practically raised.

Returning the phone to its cradle, suddenly Allison had a flashback: *She is very young, maybe three years old. Martha is speaking in a hushed, but animated, tone. Is it her father on the receiving end? She's not sure. "With all due respect, it doesn't seem right to withhold..." Martha's words halt abruptly when she notices that Allison entered the room; the male figure fades into the shadows.*

Once again, there were only fleeting moments of clarity. Why was this happening to her? It must be the stress and fatigue brought on by recent events. Either that or she's slowly going insane. *Let it go. Try to forget.*

CHAPTER 7

Silvia Sanderling spent two whole days cooking and cleaning in preparation for her sons' arrival. She hadn't seen either of them since last Thanksgiving. Simon was bringing his fiancée to meet her, and Jack, as always, would have Zavie in tow. Silvia adored Zavie, and she knew the feeling was mutual.

"Tell that boy of mine that he has had enough schooling, Zavie. Before you know it he'll be flaunting that PhD of his and he'll be too uppity for his old Mom," Silvia declared during her weekly phone conversation. "Besides, I'd like to have some grandchildren before I'm too old to enjoy them." She knew perfectly well the phone was set on "speaker" and Jack could hear every word.

"I try, Mrs. S., but he won't listen," Zavie said. "Next fall he be living in Paris and then he be too uppity for *both* of us."

"Hi, Mom!" Jack interjected in his here-we-go-again tone of voice.

"Hi, darling. I can't wait to see you in only two days. I've made all of your favorite dishes, and we'll have the best spring break ever."

"My stomach is growling already."

"Mine, too," Zavie added. "Mrs. S, did Jack tell you I sold a painting?"

"No! How wonderful! Was it a portrait or one of your gorgeous Jamaican landscapes?"

"It's titled *Caribbean Sunrise*. It sold for three hundred dollars."

"Fabulous. Congratulations, dear."

"Hey, Mom, don't forget to pick us up in Lynchburg, Saturday at 12:02, got it?" Jack said.

"How could I forget my three favorite men? So, you're meeting Simon and Carolyn at Union Station?"

"Right. I think you're going to like her, Mom. She keeps Simon in line."

"God knows I never could. I confess I'm a little nervous about meeting my baby's future wife. What if she hates me and breaks up with Simon and he never forgives…"

"Don't worry, Mom, you'll still have me."

"And me," Zavie chimed in.

"Just hurry up and come home, you two."

CHAPTER 8

Tuesday morning arrived far too quickly. The night before, more nightmares plagued Allison's sleep... *somewhere in the mansion a baby is crying. Allison tries to reach the crying infant. She climbs stairs, stairs, and more stairs. The risers grow taller and taller. Her legs become too heavy to lift...*

The alarm clock screamed at her and she woke with a jolt, feeling like she hadn't slept a wink. "This is ridiculous," she declared to an empty room. She decided to make an appointment with her physician. "Sleeping pills... that's what I need," she announced to the bathroom mirror. "Wow, those are some bags, Allie Cat. There isn't enough concealer in all of Manhattan."

Another busy day awaited Allison, and she wondered how she would get through it. Typically, she went to the gym three evenings a week, but she couldn't imagine having the energy for her work out that night. Arrangements for the annual buying trip to Paris had been in place for weeks. She and her two best fabric consultants, Natasha and Freddy, were due to leave the following Monday. Of course, Theo would accompany them. Allison wouldn't go anywhere without her trusted assistant. She even arranged for Theo's partner, James, to come along. "You haven't taken a vacation in two years. There'll be plenty of down time between shows when you and James can do some sightseeing and just relax."

The Harmon family's attorney scheduled a meeting to read Marcus's will as soon as Allison returned to the States. Why had she agreed to tackle it so soon after his death? She was still reeling from the shock of losing her beloved father suddenly and from handling the funeral arrangements. Hopefully, Dr. Bianchi would be able to fit her in this week. She couldn't continue to function on so little sleep.

As she had done for some ten years, Allison arrived at Wellington Manor promptly at six p.m. Saturday evening. As always, Martha greeted her at the front door, took her overnight bag, and ushered her young mistress into the drawing room, but nothing else about the evening was as-usual. Allison tried to prepare herself for this moment, but her father's absence was glaringly palpable. *Nothing will ever be the same*, she decided.

Marcus will never again enfold his only daughter in his adoring hug. Father and daughter will never again share a conversation. On the coffee table, where—since her eighteenth birthday—two glasses of wine always awaited them, now there was only one. Allison could not bring herself to sit opposite Marcus's favorite chair, where so many in-depth discussions occurred through the years. She picked up the glass and began to stroll about the house, experiencing anew the deep sense of loss that had been kept on hold during the past week. With so much to handle at work, she didn't have time to dwell on her sorrow or allow herself to start the all-too-inevitable grieving process.

Fortunately, Dr. Bianchi was able to fit her in for an appointment Wednesday afternoon. She prescribed a low dose of Valium to be saved "strictly for emergencies" and gave Allison a limited script for sleeping pills, warning her that they could become addictive. When Allison described her frequent nightmares and disturbing daydreams, Dr. Bianchi suggested she consider professional counseling.

"Do you think I'm going crazy, doctor?"

"You've been under a good deal of stress lately," Dr. Bianchi assured her. "Often such occurrences are a signal that the central nervous system is experiencing overload. The medication is for temporary use only. Talk therapy will be very helpful in the long term."

Wondering when she could possibly find time for psychotherapy, Allison assured Dr. Bianchi that she would schedule an appointment as soon as she returned from Paris.

Now, as she moved from room to room in the beautiful old mansion filled with antiques and memories, Allison viewed each space through new eyes. The rich walnut trim, combined with subtle earth tones on the walls and imported silk damask draperies at the windows that spanned ceiling-to-floor, created inviting warmth that could be achieved only through expert design. The home's décor paid homage to its rich history while achieving clean lines and function suitable for a modern family's lifestyle. Every rug, piece of furniture, and objet d'art had been chosen with the utmost care and exquisite taste.

When Allison's grandfather, Opa, acquired Wellington Manor from the Wellington estate in 1921, he decided to retain its original title. After his death, his wife moved to a cottage on the Hudson and the old manor was turned over to Marcus and Evelyn. Evelyn, who studied design at Yale, couldn't wait to begin renovations and turn the grand, but somewhat neglected, old "lady" into a showplace. Marcus granted his wife carte blanche to make whatever improvements she desired. Allison remembered hearing whispered hints that this project would distract her mother from a recent heartache, but she was not privy to the reason for Evelyn's sadness.

Evelyn plunged headlong into the project, starting with extensive research into the origin of the Wellington name whose history, she discovered, dated back to Field Marshal Arthur Wellesley, the First Duke of Wellington. She was even able to acquire a few original items from his estate in Ireland. Her favorite piece was the charming walnut desk that she placed in Marcus's study. With only one small drawer, it was wholly impractical; but since Marcus conducted the bulk of his business affairs in the city, he was happy to indulge his wife this extravagant, yet useless purchase.

For her final project, Evelyn had a classic Edwardian conservatory added to the rear of the home. Rising from a stone foundation with exquisite mahogany interior and gothic leaded glass windows, none but the most discerning eye could tell that the finished structure wasn't original to the home. A stone fireplace and an abundance of lush plants created interior warmth during the coldest of winters and thermally constructed, glazed windows were designed to prevent overheating in the summer.

With the inside renovations completed, Evelyn started on the surrounding property, resurrecting the stone portico at the front entrance and adding a flagstone patio and pergola to the back garden. She hired a landscape designer to create English gardens with intersecting paths and boxwood hedges that wound through the two acres of property nearly as far as the tree line along the Sound. Just beyond a sparkling pool, the rear gardens resembled a veritable park where one could wander for hours without retracing one's original path. Although Clarence was a young man when she hired him to oversee the property's maintenance, he soon realized it would take an army of workers to preserve the extensive lawns and gardens. He was given permission to hire one crew to take care of the lawns and shrubbery and another to tend the flower gardens.

The wooden gazebo in the rose garden had always been Allison's favorite spot. Octagonal in shape, it emerged from the stone wall that edged the property's western boundary. On Sundays during the summer months, she would follow the northwest path with a book in one hand and a pillow in the other. Along the inside perimeter of the gazebo ran a curved bench where Allison would position her pillow and read for hours, surrounded by the sweet scent of roses.

Each summer, Allison's twin cousins, Lydia and Lynette, would arrive from Jersey for a two week visit. Whenever they weren't lounging by the pool or romping through the gardens, the girls would spend countless hours in the gazebo, improvising plays or pretending to be fashion models on the runways of New York, London, and Paris. By the time Allison entered middle school, she had already accompanied her father and his buyers to all three locales and had learned exactly how such events were organized and executed. Quite familiar with the textile industry's lingo, she enjoyed regaling her cousins with detailed explanations regarding the weave and drape of various fabrics and their respective effects on the garment's fit.

Sometimes Martha would pack a picnic lunch for the girls and deliver it in a large wicker basket that she rolled along the gravel path in a wheel barrow borrowed from Clarence's greenhouse. It would include a thermos of freshly squeezed lemonade—to be served in china teacups—plus delicious honey ham sandwiches with just a touch of Dijon mustard and Martha's signature deviled eggs. For dessert, she might include home baked oatmeal cookies or sponge cake with fresh strawberries whenever they were in season. Allison adored the red and white checked table cloth and matching napkins reserved for such occasions. On sunny days, Martha would spread the cloth on the circular patch of soft grass that carpeted the center of the rose garden or, when it rained, on the floor of the gazebo. The girls were never given advance notice of "picnic day" nor were they allowed to request it. To preserve their sense of anticipation, Martha insisted upon surprising the girls. Much to her satisfaction, her summer picnic feasts were consistently met with enthusiastic responses.

As much as Allison enjoyed these visits from her cousins and the lazy days that accompanied them, she also relished returning to "the office" after the girls' departure. One day Allison overheard her father talking to someone on the phone. He was voicing his concerns about whether he might be expecting too much of his young daughter. "Am I forcing her to grow up too quickly? Do you think I'm denying her a carefree childhood by allowing her to shadow me at work day after day? Yes, more than anything, I want her to be happy, but what if she decides the textile industry isn't for her? Am I prepared to accept her possible pursuit of an alternate career? Suppose she meets someone and falls in love? Suppose she wants to marry and become a housewife and mother? Will I be able to let go of my dream for her future and the future of my company?"

Marcus need not have worried. Allison's focus never wavered. She never truly considered a different path. She continued to follow the trade with passion, and the day she finally called Marcus's big mahogany desk her own was marked with deep satisfaction.

CHAPTER 9

The Friday before Easter, Silvia Sanderling took a personal day from teaching. She wanted to be sure everything was in order for the arrival of her sons and their guests, especially her future daughter-in-law. With only three bedrooms, she wasn't quite sure how the sleeping arrangements should play out. She wasn't naïve enough to think that Simon and Carolyn hadn't already been sharing a bed, but she hoped they would feel awkward doing so in her home. Maybe her views were considered old fashioned by today's standards, but she just couldn't dismiss the thoroughly engrained notion that sex is a gift created by God for married couples. Finally, she decided to casually mention that the sofa in the den was available, if needed, and allow the guests to work out the assignments among themselves.

As soon as Silvia had learned that her sons would be home for the holidays—their respective spring breaks hadn't coincided for years—she arranged for the entire living area of her modest rancher to be freshly painted. Until last summer, she hadn't realized how dingy the thirty-year-old house had become. Now that Simon had graduated and landed a job, she could afford to do some updates. Last year it took all of June and most of July to complete renovations of the kitchen and the main bathroom. Next summer she would have all the carpeting replaced and the master bathroom renovated. Not that Silvia has had to shoulder the expense of tuition or books for either of her boys. Grandpa John saw to that. But she helped with their living expenses, and, in order to see them once or twice a year, she has had to spring for their train or plane tickets, as well.

What a delight it will be to have my family under one roof again. She'd been to the supermarket three times in three days, ensuring that the refrigerator and pantry were well stocked. In the deep freezer, she had casseroles of homemade lasagna, macaroni and cheese, also her famous meatloaf. On her final trip to the market, she purchased a huge Smithfield ham, just in case. She baked Simon's favorite chocolate chip cookies and Jack's favorite oatmeal raisin cookies, also an apple pie and a pumpkin pie. Zavie requested her amazing key lime pie, which she would make tomorrow. *Oh, no!* she thought. *I forgot to ask if Carolyn has any dietary requests or restrictions. What if she's one of those vegans?*

Saturday finally arrived and Silvia was ready and waiting at the station a full hour early. She could hardly wait to get her arms around those boys of hers. They may tower over her by a foot or more, but Jack and Simon would always be her "boys."

A March chill was in the air, and the weather man was calling for light snow flurries. *Snow flurries? In March? In Virginia? What's up with that?* she wondered, borrowing her fourth graders' favorite phrase. As soon as her guests are settled at home, Silvia decided she would light a fire in the cozy den, break out an abundant supply of snacks, and spend the afternoon getting reacquainted. *Whatever activities they have planned will just have to wait until Monday. The weekend is mine.*

Silvia enjoyed nothing more than gathering her family about her and listening to their banter and laughter. She never quite got used to the silence of her empty nest. Not that she sat around feeling sorry for herself. Her life was full and busy, but sometimes the evenings felt lonely, and she wondered what it might be like to have married one of numerous men who pursued her after John's death.

The train arrived on time and Silvia charged the platform, scanning back and forth for a glimpse of the anxiously anticipated quartet. Spotting their mother at the exact same moment, the two brothers rushed forward and swept her off her feet as if she were weightless. Much hugging, spinning, and squealing ensued as Zavie and Carolyn were left to guard the luggage and observe the animated scene from afar.

Finally, Zavie interrupted, feigning indignity for Silvia's benefit, "Hey, what are we? Chopped hamburger?"

"Oh, Zavie," Silvia exclaimed, out of breath. "Come here, you big, black hunk of man, and give me a hug!"

"I thought you'd never ask," Zavie responded with outstretched arms. As they embraced, Silvia's eyes finally settled on Carolyn who was standing patiently in the background, allowing the group ample time to get reacquainted.

"You must be the beautiful young woman that my Simon is going to marry. Welcome, Carolyn." Silvia took Carolyn's hands in hers, greeting her warmly as Simon made the introductions. "Her pictures don't do her justice, Simon. She's even prettier in person. Now, let's get that luggage loaded in the car and head for home. Y'all must be freezing. I ordered sunshine, but the weatherman didn't get the memo. I guess you're used to the cold by now, though…" Silvia, who talked non-stop whenever nervous or excited, ushered Carolyn toward the car. "I want to hear all about your trip, and you need to fill me in on the wedding plans. Have you picked out a gown yet? Oh, let me see that ring!" Silvia's incessant chatter accompanied the passengers all the way from the train station parking lot to her familiar back stoop in Bedford.

Then, as her anxiously awaited family settled inside the small but comfortable home, Silvia stoked the fire and "put the kettle on," as her mother and grandmother used to say. Hot cider and cocoa were brought from the kitchen, along with a generous tray of goodies. The conversation flowed freely, and Silvia Sanderling was as happy as a flea on a dog.

Easter Sunday dawned sunny, but cold. Of course, Silvia's houseguests had come prepared to attend the church service, but they weren't expecting to need winter coats. Jack and Simon had always attended church. Silvia saw to that, and they never questioned the expectation, at least not more than once. Silvia knew if she were to successfully raise two boys by herself, she would have to be both strong and strict. At an early age, her boys discovered that certain issues, like going to church, were non-negotiable. When they were younger, the Sanderling brothers sang in the choir and played hand bells, too. Jack couldn't speak for his brother on the subject, but he actually enjoyed the services, especially at Easter and Christmas.

Today, the chancel would be filled with fragrant Easter Lilies; Pastor Davis would give a dynamic, but not-too-judgmental sermon; and the music director would pull out all the stops. In addition to a brass quartet hired from the Roanoke Symphony, the worshippers could expect glorious organ music, and a special anthem or cantata, all prepared to entice the twice-a-year attendees to start coming to church regularly.

The service did not disappoint. Afterwards, they stopped at the Bedford cemetery to lay flowers on the graves of John and Ellen Sanderling and their son, John II. Then, with everyone's help, Silvia prepared a sumptuous spread of baked ham, sweet potato casserole, green beans, home-made yeast rolls and pie a la mode. Much to Silvia's delight, Carolyn joined in the preparations with ease, and ate as heartily as the men. Silvia could imagine nothing more idyllic than having her family gathered at the dining room table to break bread together on Easter Sunday, especially now that Simon was getting married in June and Jack was scheduled to spend the fall semester in France.

CHAPTER 10

Ordinarily, the president of H & H would avoid both the madness of Fashion Week in Paris and the biannual buying trips. Long ago Marcus had entrusted this onerous duty to capable subordinates. However, during the first year of Allison's official presidency, she deemed it important to personally reinforce relationships with both suppliers and designers worldwide. The Paris scene would provide an effective platform for firmly establishing her standing in the international arena. Besides, she really needed to get away, far away. Perhaps a different locale would help her shake off those disturbing thoughts and dreams that continued to surface.

Over the years, Allison had become an expert at packing for overseas flights. She kept a makeup bag at-the-ready with regulation size shampoo, conditioner, shower gel, and duplicates of her foundation, blush, lipstick, and mascara. Her travel clothes consisted of wrinkle resistant fabrics which she rolled, rather than folded, both to prevent creases and to fit everything into a single suitcase. She even managed to fit into one tiny compartment two crepe evening gowns—one black, the other mauve—and a pair of folding evening shoes, along with a wrinkle free shawl.

Because Harmon & Harmon's private jet would surely attract more attention than she was ready to encounter, Allison opted to travel by commercial airliner. She hoped she wouldn't be recognized by the paparazzi and that reporters would leave her and her entourage alone on this trip. She had no problem with ordinary, legitimate reporters, and she regularly scheduled press conferences to keep them abreast of newsworthy information about the company. Just last week, she held a lengthy press conference, inviting all of the usual representatives to attend. She thanked them for having preserved the dignity of her father's funeral proceedings and allowed them to question her at liberty and take photographs until they were satisfied.

Early in his career, Marcus wisely established mutually respectful relationships with the major newspaper publishers and television reporters in the city. When she was quite young, he taught his daughter how to deal with the media. "The press can be our greatest ally," he told her, "but we must always be in control of what information is released to the public and how it is presented. If public figures are honest and forthright, the press will come to trust us and, in turn, will respect our right to some privacy in our personal lives. If we avoid the press, they may think we're trying to hide something and will, consequently, invade our privacy."

For the most part Marcus had been correct, but the paparazzi, Allison soon discovered, were excluded from Marcus's respect and were most certainly not entitled to his confidences. He had seen too many high profile businesses and famous families destroyed by these scandal seeking photographers. Now, with her father's death, she realized she would become the primary target of tabloid interest and surveillance, but she hoped and prayed for just a little more time to fully process her recent life altering event. In the meantime, it was her responsibility to keep the company stable and viable, and that was best accomplished by traveling to Paris as inconspicuously as possible.

The group decided to adopt the persona of college students studying abroad. Since all five travelers appeared youthful, the donning of blue jeans, baseball caps, and backpacks created a convincing ruse. Allison completed the disguise by forgoing makeup, a trick she learned by observing various celebrities in the entertainment industry.

After a long, uneventful flight—most of which Allison slept through—she and her staff arrived at Charles De Gaulle where a car was waiting to take them to the hotel. On his trips to Paris, Marcus always stayed at Le Meurice, but Theo, at Allison's request, reserved three suites at a less opulent lodging, thus further confusing the paparazzi, she hoped. Theo handled all transactions requiring identification, which allowed the others to check in under false identities. Allison was confident that primary attention would be focused on the prominent hotels in the vicinity of the Louvre-Tuileries district and on the super models, famous designers, and movie stars in attendance.

Tomorrow, the H & H group planned to travel via Métro to further avoid notice. Once they arrived at each venue, Allison would locate the ladies' room, change clothes quickly, and apply makeup. It was important for her to frequent as many shows as possible during Fashion Week, but with the help of her counterfeit backstage press pass, she planned to avoid the red carpet scene altogether.

Of course, H & H must remain attentive to the latest haute couture if the enterprise was to thrive. The front-line fashion industry was the company's bread-and-butter, so to speak—especially in the French and Italian markets. Allison must be a visible presence at Saint Laurent, Versace, Dior, and Chanel, among others, but on her own time, she intended to remain anonymous. Truthfully, she found the whole Fashion Week scene to be pretentious, even a bit repulsive. Schmoozing with the elite set was not her favorite activity, but ultimately a certain amount of networking was necessary in her business. Fortunately, Natasha and Freddy relished the bustling excitement and had become well regarded among their peers in the industry. They could be trusted to represent H & H at all future international events.

In meetings with her father, Allison always emphasized the importance of serving the masses. She convinced him that, while expensive fabrics like silk charmeuse, bouclé tweed, and Armani herringbone dominated the runways, they were inaccessible to the average consumer. So, once she made an appearance at the main runway shows, she would check out the shops lining Rue Popincourt to the north. According to Natasha, a single day spent exploring the boutiques along that one narrow street could produce more accurate research than a whole week of runway shows and after-parties.

By Thursday, Allison was exhausted from dealing with crowds, bright lights, too many late nights, and too much champagne. She felt like she had changed clothes more often than the runway models. She rose early—during Fall Fashion Week in Paris, eight a.m. was considered *very* early. She donned her student-traveling-abroad disguise, left a note under Theo's door, and walked to the nearest Métro station. Within thirty minutes she arrived at the Saint-Ambroise stop, a few blocks north of her destination. She longed to escape traffic noise and crowds of people just for a few hours. She decided to head for Square Maurice Gardette, a small park where she could take a quiet, relaxing stroll along the tree lined path. But first, a quick stop at L'Arté Café on Rue du Général Renault promised a perfect cup of strong coffee to clear the morning cobwebs.

Despite the cool temperature and brisk breeze, the sun shined brightly, warming Allison's skin as the coffee heated her insides. In the park, trees shed in preparation for winter dormancy. With each gust of wind, dancing leaves of varying shapes and colors swirled about the young woman's feet, and she rejoiced in this flawless autumn morning. The park, with its crisscrossing paths and abundance of joggers and dog walkers, felt like a miniature version of Central Park. By the time she completed two revolutions, her coffee cup was nearly empty and she was ready to take off her outerwear. She sat on a bench and removed her backpack and sweat shirt.

The walk accomplished its purpose, leaving Allison refreshed and clear headed. As she swallowed the final drops of an excellent French Roast, she remembered that a clear head can be both a blessing and a curse. For the first time since arriving in Paris, she had time to think about something other than couture, and thinking meant remembering or conjuring or whatever antics her mind had been engaging in lately.

Allie is four or five years old. Mommy and Daddy are talking in the garden just below her bedroom window. "I need to see him, Marc. Please try to understand how important this is to me."

"Evie, Sweetheart, you know that wouldn't be wise. Please try to let it go."

Mommy's voice rises in volume: "It was a mistake, Marc. We shouldn't have allowed your father to bully us."

At this moment, Allison surmised, *Daddy must have noticed my open window.* "Sh! Evie, lower your voice. Allie will hear us. Come inside. We'll talk in the library."

Talk about what, Allison wondered. *Who did her mother want to see?* She was convinced this was no daydream. No, this was a real memory, not her imagination, not a hallucination. Now she realized she was remembering real events and conversations from her childhood. What was the secret that her parents kept from her as a child? Why did her father continue to shield her from it as an adult? Now that Marcus was gone, how would she ever uncover the truth?

At that moment, Allison resolved to unravel the mystery. She would start as soon as she returned to the States. "Psychotherapy, my eye. What I need is a private detective," she mumbled.

"Pardon?" a male voice responded in French. Lost in her own thoughts, she hadn't noticed the young man sharing her bench at the opposite end.

"Oh, je suis désolé!" she apologized, then breaking into a combination of English and French, added, "I was just… penseé, um, thinking out loud."

"Ah, you speak English," he interrupted, sounding relieved. "Are you American?"

"Yes. I'm sorry if I disturbed your work," she answered, nodding at his laptop. "Sometimes I think out loud. It's a bad habit."

"It's okay. I was getting nowhere, anyway."

"Are you from New York?" she asked, pointing at his I-Heart-New-York computer bag.

"I guess you could say I'm a transplanted New Yorker. I'm a student."

"Really? Small world. What are you working on, if you don't mind my asking?"

"I don't mind. It's my dissertation. My revisions are due in a few weeks and I'm totally stuck. So, you're from New York?"

"Born and bred... a Long Island girl." Allison noticed that this young man was quite easy on the eyes and, surprising herself, wished she had worn makeup and styled her hair.

"This is going to sound like a line, but you look familiar. Have we met before?"

"No, I don't think so, and yes, it does sound like a line, a very stale line at that," she joked.

"I warned you, but you really do look familiar. Do you go to the Academy of Fine Arts? Maybe I've seen you on campus."

"Columbia, here," she answered, holding up her sweatshirt with the CU emblem embossed across the front. "So, what's your paper about? How to pick up girls in Paris?" she teased.

"If I'm not mistaken, you spoke first," he countered, playfully.

"Touché, monsieur!"

"It's supposed to be about French Art History and the influence of the French masters on American artists. I've spent weeks visiting all of the art galleries and libraries in Paris. I've done hours and hours of research and made pages and pages of notes, but I can't seem to pull it all together."

"It sounds like a classic case of information-overload to me," Allison said.

"Oh? And what does the doctor prescribe for this condition? By the way, does the doctor have a name?"

"Allie," she said, suddenly feeling shy and wondering why she allowed a conversation with a complete stranger to progress this far. "I recommend taking a break."

"An excellent suggestion. My name is Jack, Jack Sanderling. Enchanté, Allie." Jack half-stood, moved closer, and offered his right hand while balancing the laptop with his left.

"Enchanté," she answered shyly as she accepted his hand. It felt warm and soothing.

Now what? Allison wondered. *Now that we've introduced ourselves, what happens next?* For an almost-thirty-year-old, she was sorely inexperienced in the flirting department. *Should I walk away and risk never seeing him again?* She was strangely attracted to this man who, instead of returning to the opposite end of the bench, was now sitting close enough that she could smell his aftershave. It smelled like a mixture of nutmeg and Irish Spring soap. She liked it.

"What brings you to Paris, Allie?" Jack asked.

Whew! Rescued from the nearly-awkward silence, she sighed. *But how much should I reveal about myself? He already thinks he's seen me before.* She didn't like deceit but decided it was safest to maintain her college-student persona. She had experienced the paparazzi enough to know they could pop up anywhere, at any time. It would be so much easier and less stressful to complete her assignment in Paris without constantly having to deal with rude photographers.

"A group of us from Columbia decided to travel abroad," she lied.

"You seem to have lost your group," he said, gesturing in a circle.

"They wanted to sleep in this morning. I left them at the hotel."

"I see."

"I'm used to walking in the morning, so I decided to look for a park."

"Can I, uh... may I interest you in a cup of café délicieux? There's an excellent café just around the corner."

"Merci, but I just—"

"They have tables outside, so we can enjoy this beautiful weather," Jack interrupted.

"Actually, that sounds great." Allison realized her opportunity for a graceful exit had just passed, but she felt an odd sense of ease in this stranger's presence. Sure, he was attractive, with his thick, dark hair and gorgeous blue eyes, but his casual, playful manner was what intrigued her. Besides, she had been lonely since her father's death and having someone to talk to felt comforting.

Allison had only allowed herself to date a mere handful of guys since college, fearing a serious relationship might distract her from her all-consuming career. Besides, she was never able to trust that a man was interested in her for herself and not her wealth. She thrived on the work that she knew inside and out, and she became successful because of her focus and fervent drive to be the best in her field. Being born into the company required more work, not less. Her entire life had been devoted to her career, and she expended a good deal of energy to earn the respect of colleagues, customers, and employees alike, and to prove her competence. Never let it be said that Allison Harmon gained her position through nepotism.

CHAPTER 11

Together, Jack and Allison strolled to the nearby café, enjoying the cool breeze and each other's company. Jack acted like a true gentleman, taking her elbow as they crossed the street and pulling her chair out once they reached the outdoor tables.

"How do you take your coffee?" he asked.

"One sugar, please."

As Jack turned to enter the café, Allison studied his gait, observing his confident yet unassuming manner. Drawing upon a course in Kinesics that she had taken as an undergraduate, she remembered that one can tell a lot about a person's personality and character by the way he carries himself. Jack's body language was open and easy-going, indicating authenticity and self-confidence.

Nearly two hours passed like the blink of an eye before Allison thought to check the time. "Good grief!" she exclaimed, glancing at her phone. "My phone is dead. Do you have the time?"

"We might as well order lunch now. It's almost noon," Jack said, checking his watch.

"Oh, no! I need to get back. It'll soon be time to… I need to go."

"Please stay," he implored, reaching for her hand.

His hand rested on top of hers, and, for an instant, she made no effort to remove it. What was it about this man that intrigued and paralyzed her? His clear blue eyes were definitely mesmerizing, but it was more than just his good looks that attracted her. He was easy to talk to and refreshingly unpretentious, and his southern accent was charming. She enjoyed the way he teased her without malice. Somehow she managed to get acquainted with this interesting man without revealing her true identity. She talked about her father's recent passing and how difficult it was to adjust to being alone, especially since her mother died when she was a child. In order to protect her identity, she drew upon memories of her time as a student at Columbia, never once mentioning she was the CEO of the largest, most lucrative textile industry in the world.

Jack shared his background about growing up near the mountains of Virginia without a father, his love of art, his famous grandfather, and how awkward he felt upon first arriving in Manhattan. He described life in a small town, referring to his mother with such respect that Allison felt genuinely moved. He told Allison about his best friend, Zavie Johnson, and how the young, talented Jamaican had quickly made a name for himself in the States as an artist. She mentioned that her father took her to Jamaica for her thirteenth birthday and how much they both admired the native artwork.

"The colors are so vibrant," she exclaimed. "Daddy bought a beautiful painting that still hangs in his office."

Once Allison was convinced she wanted to get to know Jack, she felt guilty about misrepresenting herself, but there wasn't enough time to remedy the situation.

"I'm sorry. I really can't stay," Allison insisted, regaining her equilibrium. She stood quickly, scraping the wrought iron chair noisily across the brick terrace. For the first time in her life she felt the temptation to throw caution to the wind. *I should retreat quickly before I change my mind.* "How about tomorrow? Could we meet again tomorrow?"

"Of course, but where… when?"

Allison was already moving in the direction of the Métro station.

"Ten o'clock, same place," she called back to him. Tomorrow she would tell him the truth about her identity.

"Wait—I don't even know your last name!" But she disappeared around the corner, and Jack was left with a sinking feeling that he would likely never see this enchanting Allie-person again.

CHAPTER 12

Allison rushed into the hotel lobby at nearly one thirty p.m., where Theo was pacing frantically.

"Where have you been?" he asked, obviously panicked.

"I know, I'm sorry. I lost track of the time," she answered, rushing past him to catch the elevator. He followed on her heels.

"I've been calling you for an hour or more. We only have a few minutes to get to the meeting across town."

"I know, I know. I forgot to charge my phone last night. Listen, call a cab while I grab my clothes. I'll meet you out front in five."

By some miracle and with the help of a speeding taxi driver, they arrived at the meeting only a few minutes late. Fortunately, Freddy and Natasha preceded them and set up the preliminary presentation, so their tardy entrance was barely noticeable. Still, Allison felt guilty for being so uncharacteristically irresponsible and for worrying Theo. The meeting, however, was a huge success, landing Harmon & Harmon a major contract with Versace. Later, she could explain to Theo what—or rather who—detained her.

That evening, for the first time since arriving in Paris, Allison and her entourage were hounded by aggressive reporters, especially upon leaving the Chanel show and the after-party. By the time the group finally returned to the hotel, it was past one a.m. Allison was relieved that tomorrow evening's events would cap off Fashion Week. She decided to take a sleeping pill, but not to prevent nightmares. If anything kept her awake tonight, it would be anticipation about seeing Jack again. As she waited for the pill to take effect, she relived every moment of the morning's encounter and realized she had never been attracted to a man in this way before. For the first time, she longed to spend more time with a man, and she was pretty sure he felt the same way about her.

The H & H group was scheduled to fly back to New York Saturday afternoon, but first, she knew she had to make sure a plan was in place for continuing to see Jack Sanderling.

CHAPTER 13

Jack pulled out his laptop and tried to work on his paper, but he couldn't concentrate. Allie had gotten under his skin. It was more than her well-toned body and flawless complexion despite no evidence of makeup. Her eyes—were they brown or hazel?—pulled him deep into her soul, especially when she spoke of her father, whom she obviously adored. Jack loved the way her bushy ponytail fanned out from the opening at the back of her baseball cap, twisting in the wind. But beyond the physical attraction, he found her innocence refreshing. Most of the women he had met in New York were street-wise and forward, but Allie's demeanor struck him as natural and unassuming, yet somehow sophisticated. *She's intriguing, that's for sure.* He could hardly wait to see her again tomorrow.

After repeated attempts at composing the same paragraph, Jack decided to go to a library. Maybe a change of scenery would help him get back on track. Recalling that Rue de Louvois was a short Métro ride away, he headed for Bibliothéque Nationale de France where he spent the afternoon trying unsuccessfully to concentrate on his paper. Finally, he decided to call it a day. He stopped for a light supper at his favorite bistro and caught a movie—with English subtitles—before heading back to the hostel that had been his home-away-from-home for the past two months.

When Jack finally returned to the boardinghouse, it was after ten p.m. A few of his fellow students were gathered around the television in the lobby, watching the news. As usual, it was focused on the events of Fashion Week, which didn't interest him in the least. But the gorgeous young woman in the stunning evening gown caught his eye. *She looks so familiar. I think I know her. Wait—No, it can't be...*

Even after living in Paris for two months, Jack's command of the French language was lacking, but he moved closer to the TV and listened intently, trying to catch any familiar words or phrases that might confirm or deny his unlikely suspicion.

"Le fille du Mogol textile américain, Marcus Harmon a été repérée quittant le défilé Chanel ce soir portant de Lourdes Atencio," *The daughter of the American textile mogul, Marcus Harmon, was spotted exiting the Chanel fashion show this evening,* "en mauve, parfaitement accentuée par les bijoux de famille Harmon." *wearing Lourdes Atencio, in mauve, perfectly accentuated by Harmon family jewels.*

I really do have Allie on the brain, Jack chided himself. *Now I'm beginning to conjure her. I need to go to bed.* He turned to walk away, convinced that the exquisitely dressed vision on the screen couldn't possibly be his Allie from that morning. But the announcer's next sentence stopped him in his tracks.

"Des sources indiquent que Allison Harmon a été dans Paris toute la semaine, mais a réussi à échapper à la presse jusqu'à ce soir." *Sources indicate that Allison Harmon has been in Paris all week, but has managed to evade the press until this evening.*

Nearly dropping his laptop on the floor, Jack sank into the nearest chair, his eyes never leaving the screen.

"Le jeune Harmon Mme a été à la tête de Harmon & Harmon entreprises depuis la retraite de l'Harmon aîné il y a deux ans." *The young Ms. Harmon has been at the helm of Harmon & Harmon Enterprises since the elder Harmon's retirement two years ago.* "Avec la mort récente de son père, elle possède maintenant l'entreprise de plusieurs milliards de dollars qui fournit des textiles à la plupart des sociétés de conception majeur du monde," *With her father's recent death, she now owns the multi-billion-dollar firm that supplies textiles to most of the world's major design companies.*

"What the hell!" Jack exclaimed. "It *is* her. She lied to me." Jack had never been one to cuss. He was raised to believe that profanity was indicative of ignorance and laziness. But he couldn't help himself. For the first time since high school he found a woman that interested him—someone he actually wanted to get to know better—and she turned out to be a liar, a total fake. Suddenly aware that everyone in the room was staring at him, he stood and beat a hasty retreat up the stairs.

"…and to think I actually wasted a whole afternoon thinking about her," he said aloud to an empty room. He dropped to the foot of his bed, feeling betrayed and utterly alone. "I need to talk to Zavie," he decided.

CHAPTER 14

The next morning, Allison awoke early despite another late night. She was energized by the prospect of seeing Jack and hoped she could travel to their meeting place without being noticed. Now that her cover had been blown, it would be hard to move about the city unnoticed. She had to get to Jack before he saw the morning paper. She needed to explain why she deceived him about her identity. Most of all, she needed to lay her eyes on this man that caused her insides to melt like warm Jell-O. She hoped the reporters hadn't camped out in the lobby. As far as she could tell, they didn't follow her back to the hotel last night. Cleverly, Theo led the paparazzi to Le Meurice, and then Allison ducked out the back entrance where a taxi was waiting to take her to her real hotel.

She dressed quickly, but took the time to put on a bit of lipstick and blush. Instead of a sweatshirt with her jeans, she pulled on a blouse and navy wool blazer. Today, she must take care to be herself... not Allison Harmon, the famous tycoon or Allison Harmon, the wealthy heiress. Today, she longed to be Allie, an average woman of twenty-seven who has finally met a man who interests her.

Just to be safe, she took the back stairs down to the employee's entrance and slipped out unnoticed. The morning was clear, chilly, and full of promise. Rounding the corner toward the Métro station, she wrapped her scarf around her neck, checking back toward the hotel to be sure she hadn't been spotted. Not until she was safely seated on the train did she allow herself to enjoy the ever-increasing excitement. Positively giddy with anticipation, she wished she weren't returning to New York without Jack. Waiting until January to see him again would be agonizing.

Finally, Allison got off at the same stop as yesterday and headed for the park. The wind picked up speed, and her hair, which she wore loosely about her shoulders, began to whip in all directions. She pulled the scarf around her head and picked up her pace. Her heart pounded wildly in anticipation of the meeting.

Would he be seated on *their* bench? Or would he go to the café? Oh, dear, they hadn't specified, had they? They should have exchanged phone numbers. She should have kept better track of the time so they could have made more definite plans for today's rendezvous. Not one to let panic overtake her, Allison decided to walk back and forth between the two potential meeting spots so she couldn't possibly miss him.

Ten minutes passed, then twenty, then thirty. No sign of Jack. She couldn't have missed him. She'd arrived plenty early. Even if he had preceded her, he wouldn't have left before the appointed time. It took a mere three to four minutes to walk from the park to the café. She would have spotted him at one or the other location. The truth began to sink in. Either Jack had changed his mind about wanting to see her again, or he never intended to meet her in the first place.

How could she have been so naïve? How could she have totally missed the signals? *He's the one who was so anxious to arrange another meeting. Maybe he overslept. Maybe he missed the subway. He doesn't even know my last name, so how could he possibly contact me to let me know he's running late? It serves me right for being deceitful.*

Now confused and despondent, Allison decided to order a cup of coffee and start the process of trying to forget Jack Sanderling. She returned to the hotel in a daze, not caring if she was recognized, not caring about anything. She passed through the lobby to the elevator, totally unaware that people were staring at her and whispering her name. Fortunately, no one approached her.

She had exactly one hour to finish packing before the car arrived to take the H & H group to the airport. She went through the motions, feeling confused, disappointed, and foolish. Once that plane took off, she planned on leaving both the City of Love and all thoughts of Jack Sanderling behind her for good.

CHAPTER 15

Entering the terminal at LaGuardia, Allison was bombarded by reporters firing questions at her about the Paris shows. Her cover was blown, and if she hoped to travel incognito in the future, she'd have to come up with a new disguise. Theo tried to intervene, but Allison, grateful for the distraction, decided to give a statement. She didn't even care that she would appear in the media looking like she just rolled out of bed. She could picture the headline:

"New York Textile Tycoon Returns from Paris Fashion Scene Looking like Something the Cat Dragged In."

When the reporters and photographers followed the H & H group to baggage claim and then outside to the waiting limousine, however, Theo became visibly irritated by their attention. He insisted they back off, but Allison didn't care. She felt numb, just wanting to get home and go to bed. She planned to sleep all day Sunday and dive into work with a vengeance Monday morning. She also intended to hire a private detective to delve into her family's suspicious history. It had become evident that her parents kept something significant from her, and she wouldn't rest until she uncovered what was intentionally unrevealed throughout her entire life. Perhaps a long talk with Martha was in order.

CHAPTER 16

Jack decided that women were simply not worth the trouble they always seemed to cause. He never should have allowed himself to be attracted to Allison Harmon. He had goals to accomplish and a career to establish. *Stay focused, Sanderling. Finish your dissertation,* he told himself. *In a few months you'll be done. By January you'll be back in New York, starting the career that you've dreamed about forever.* Talking to Zavie didn't really help, either. Zavie had found the love of his life. Zavie, who opened a studio in Greenwich Village, had quickly established himself as a prominent artist. Zavie had it all together. His advice to give Allie a chance—to give love a chance—seemed naive to Jack.

He doesn't get how betrayed I feel by her lack of trust in me. I'd be crazy to pursue a relationship that started as a lie, wouldn't I? She was just toying with me, anyway. A woman in her position, with her wealth and prestige, probably plays with men's feelings all the time just for a lark. I don't need her. I don't need that kind of grief. Just forget about her.

Occasionally, Jack recalled Simon's wedding from the previous summer. He remembered how blissfully happy Simon and Carolyn looked as they recited their vows and later during their first dance as husband and wife. Whenever he and Simon talked, married life seemed to suit his younger brother. He and Carolyn were even talking about starting a family. Jack hadn't given up on the possibility of a lasting relationship, but he would approach women much more cautiously in the future, and certainly not anytime soon.

With new resolve, Jack focused all of his energy on completing his fellowship and earning his PhD. But at night, lying in bed, he couldn't erase the vision of Allie's face with that warm, inviting smile and those engaging brown eyes that betrayed an underlying shyness. *Was it all just an act?* He remembered her ponytail billowing in the breeze, and that compact, athletic body. Most of all he remembered how easy she was to talk to. He really opened up to this woman. That's when the anger would start to rise in his throat. *Who knows how much of what she said was actually true? Maybe her entire story was nothing more than a ruse.*

CHAPTER 17

"You've handled my father's personal affairs for many years, Zach. Have you ever noticed anything of a suspicious nature?" Allison paced back and forth nervously in front of her desk where Zachary Grayson was seated before her in one of two upholstered chairs. Typically, she would keep personal and professional matters separate. A reading of Marcus's will was scheduled for Friday evening at the Manor, but Allison had called Zachary Grayson to her downtown office. Since returning from Paris, she has been plagued by a strange foreboding and a determination to uncover the mystery of her childhood.

"What do mean by 'suspicious'?" Zachary asked.

"You know—something out of the ordinary. Listen, Zach, I don't want any surprises on Friday. I don't want to suddenly discover that my father was having an affair or that he had a gambling addiction and gambled away the family fortune. I sense he was hiding something, and I'd rather find out about it now."

"Ms. Harmon, I can assure you everything is in order," Zach insisted. "You, of course, are his sole beneficiary, and the estate is very much intact."

"Hmm." Allison placed a finger to her chin and continued to pace. "What about any unusual expenditures?"

"You'd have to run that by John," Zachary answered. John Farber was the accountant who handled Marcus's personal finances for many years. "I'll read over everything again, but as far as I can tell, the will is straightforward. I certainly would have informed you if I'd found anything amiss."

"Of course. I understand, Zach. It's just that… I've been having these flashes of memory lately." Allison moved to the window where she stared at something in the distance. "Memories from my childhood, you know, and I just wondered…" Turning to face Zach, she leaned against the windowsill.

"Thank you for coming, Zach. I appreciate it." Allison moved toward him with her right hand outstretched. "I'll see you Friday evening, okay?"

"Yes, seven p.m., right?" Zach stood. Shaking his hand, Allison said, "Right. Have a good day." As Allison ushered him out, she instructed Theo to get John Farber on the phone.

"Don't forget, Miss Harmon, you have a meeting with Bridges in ten minutes."

"Yes, right. See if John can meet me for lunch. Jean Georges at noon. No, make it one. Tell him I'm paying… and you'd better make a reservation."

"Will do," Theo answered, but Allison had already closed the door. *Theo can see how distracted I've been since we returned from Paris. I'm glad I told him about meeting a guy in the park, but I wish I hadn't let Jack get to me like this. I can't let him affect my work or the trust of my staff.*

Allison opened the door a crack and peeped out. "…and call me a cab, please."

CHAPTER 18

Jack was anxious to get home—funny how easily he now called New York City "home". Only a few years earlier, he had felt totally out of his element there. Of course, Bedford will always be his home town, but there wasn't much in the way of entertainment or opportunity there. He remembered feeling interminably restless as a teenager, especially before earning his driver's license. Finally, he and his friends could take turns driving to Lynchburg or Roanoke on the weekends.

Living in Paris for four months was an adventure, to be sure, and his command of the language improved immensely. Not only can he order a complete meal without the garçon looking at him like he had two heads, but he can ask for help in any library or museum with successful results. If he hadn't been a poverty-stricken student, he might even have managed to sample the incredible cuisine and delectable wine for which France was famous. He resolved to return one day as Dr. Jack Sanderling, the Art History expert, and correct that omission.

Only a few hours ago, he had ceremoniously pressed "send" and submitted his completed dissertation to his advisor in America. Within the month, he would stand before a panel of jurists to defend it and finally the long, arduous process would come to an end. He thought about how proud both his father and his grandfather would have been by his accomplishment and wished he could share it with them. Of course, Silvia would be present for the "hooding" ceremony. She had already planned to spend her Christmas break in New York. Her excitement was infectious and caused Jack to beam with pride. The last time they talked, she had prattled on about how she wanted to see a Broadway play, go shopping at Prada (just to look, of course) and take a carriage ride through Central Park.

"...and of course, I want to see Zavie's studio and meet his girlfriend. Most of all, I can't wait to see my son, the doctor. Sweetheart, are you all right? You've hardly said two words."

"Well, Mom, it's kind of hard to get a word in."

"I know, I get carried away when I'm excited, but you seem down. Are you okay?"

"I'm fine, Mom, just tired and ready to go home."

"I'll bet you are! It won't be long now. You hang in there, and I'll see you on the twenty-seventh."

The conversation ended with their characteristic "love-yous," abbreviated, as usual, by concern that it would cost a fortune to continue their oversees call beyond a few minutes.

As much as he resented Allison Harmon—wishing he had never met her—Jack credited her with the intense determination with which he has plunged into his work during the past month and a half. Every time she popped into his mind, he would adopt an even greater resolve to focus on his research and final revisions. Each morning at around ten, he indulged the overwhelming urge to run as fast and far as he could until his body submitted to exhaustion, but his mind felt amazingly invigorated. Then, and only then, was he able to successfully accomplish six to eight straight hours of the mental aerobics necessary to complete his daunting task. Sometimes he would forget to eat until his stomach growled audibly, compelling him to leave the library, only to discover it had grown dark outside. By the way his clothes were fitting, he knew he had lost weight, but he didn't care. Soon he would leave Paris and its ghosts behind. Soon he would begin a new life and career, neither of which included Allison Harmon.

Jack had already submitted his resume to several museums and art galleries in New York, Pittsburg, and Cleveland, and his advisor recommended that he check out potential teaching positions, as well. To appease Dr. Devlin, Jack applied reluctantly to a few universities, but he had no intention of becoming a college professor. Besides the fact that he had enough of academia to last a lifetime, he couldn't imagine sharing such mind-altering revelations with snotty-nosed college students, some of whom perhaps had no real passion for art, who were simply taking up space in a classroom until they could decide what or who they wanted to become. Almost-Doctor Jack Sanderling spent his entire adulthood earning the privilege of sharing space with the universe's finest works of art, inhaling the sweet perfume of greatness. He earned the right to step into any canvas and vicariously experience each stroke as if it were his own, to feel the wet clay of the sculptor ooze between his fingers as he caressed it into perfect form. Such intimacy must be reserved for only the most fervent devotees.

What would he do for the next two weeks until he boarded the plane for LaGuardia? How would he keep his mind occupied? More specifically, how would he keep from letting Allison creep from the far recesses to the forefront? Without the diversion of his paper, he feared losing the battle he had been fighting for nearly two months.

What he needed to erase the memory of Allison, he decided, is another woman. Now he would have time to focus on meeting someone, but whom? Chelsea, a fellow student from the hostel? She seemed interested. What about that pretty French fille from Le Bistro du Halle where he bought his coffee every morning? She definitely flirted with him. No. Long distance romances were simply not practical.

Wait! Who says it has to be a romance? Why not just a two-week fling? A distraction with no strings attached.

CHAPTER 19

Allison resolved to talk to Martha after the reading of her father's will, especially since her lunch meeting with John Farber revealed nothing suspect about Marcus's personal finances. There were numerous tax shelters about which she had known nothing, but Marcus had always been both generous with his wealth and smart about investments. John assured her that her father's unwavering support of such organizations as the American Red Cross, the Salvation Army, the Children's Hospital of New York, plus his Alma Mater and various scholarship funds was long-standing and uninterrupted. There were trust funds for his loyal staff and for any of Allison's progeny. John had personally handled all charity transactions and investments, and upon Marcus's retirement two years ago, submitted the books for an exhaustive audit.

"Believe me, Allison, the IRS watches accounts like your father's very closely," John asserted. "If anything were out of order, they would be all over me in a heartbeat."

"Of course, John. I trust you completely, just as Daddy did. I'm simply curious about some events from my childhood and thought maybe the accounts might shed some light." Well, that was that.

If there were any significance to her strange memories, surely Martha could clarify them. Allison was aware that children, with their vivid imaginations, tended to give conversations and events more import than they warranted. Perhaps the grief of losing her mother at such an early age caused her imagination to work overtime. *If only I could talk to Daddy about this*, she thought. *If only I had shared my thoughts and concerns with him before he… I still can't believe he's gone. I miss him so much.*

She also missed Jack Sanderling, that lovely—okay, sexy—man whom she met in Paris. At times, she imagined what he might say if she were to share the details of her family's drama, real or imagined. Unlike many men—certainly the few men she dated—he was a good listener. Why did she even care? After he stood her up and essentially disappeared into thin air, she should just forget about him. After all, it was only a cup of coffee and a brief conversation that they shared. She'll never see him again, and she should be able to erase him from her memory bank. So, how did he manage to keep shoving himself back into her pathetic mind? Why did she think she saw him at least once a week on the street or in a restaurant? *You're a hopeless romantic, Allie. What woman wouldn't fall instantly in love with a gorgeous man that she met in the City of Love? Delete, delete, delete.*

CHAPTER 20

Felix had the Mercedes waiting for Allison promptly at five thirty p.m. Because of the typical Friday afternoon traffic, it would take more than the usual forty-five minutes to get from Manhattan to their destination on Long Island. Allison asked Martha to prepare drinks and heavy hors d'oeuvres for the meeting and to expect her to spend Friday night at the Manor instead of her usual Saturday.

The trip took nearly an hour, during which Allison refreshed her makeup and sent a few text messages. She was still trying to catch up at work after her week away from the office. She also took the opportunity to ask Felix a few questions.

"I know my father considered you a friend as well as an employee, Felix. He would have trusted you to keep any confidences, right?"

"Yes, Miss. I 'spect he would," Felix responded, addressing her through the rear view mirror.

"I was wondering," Allison continued. "Do you remember anything he might have wanted to keep from me, maybe something he thought I was too young to understand? Now that he's gone, I think it would be okay to share any secrets with me. After all, now that I'm to inherit his entire estate, I have a right to know everything, don't you agree?"

"Yes, Miss, but I don't recall anything, in particular."

"Did he ever ask you to drive him anywhere out of the ordinary?"

"No, Miss, not that I recall. What are you gettin' at?"

"Nothing, really. It's just that some strange memories have been surfacing, and I'd like to sort them out. If you think of anything, anything at all, will you let me know?"

"Yes, Miss, 'course I will."

"Thank you, Felix."

"Matter o' fact, Miss, I been wonderin' somethin' too," Felix added tentatively.

"Oh? What is it?"

"Well, now that Mr. Harmon's gone, and you don't need drivin' around much, I been wonderin' if you've been thinkin' you might not need ol' Felix anymore."

"Well, that depends," Allison said. "Does Martha still need you to drive her for errands and groceries?"

"Yes, I 'spect so."

"Do you still take care of the vehicles and the garage?"

"Yes. I try my best."

"Do you help Martha and Gretchen with odd jobs in the house and lend a hand with dinner parties?"

"Yes."

"Do you like your job?"

"Yes, Miss."

"Do I pay you enough?"

"Oh, yes, Miss Allison, you pay me plenty."

"Okay, then, as far as I'm concerned, the job is yours as long as I own Wellington Manor."

"Was you thinkin' o' sellin'?" Felix asked.

"I haven't made a decision about it one way or the other, and I won't be ready to for quite some time. I promise to give you plenty of notice before making any major changes. Okay?"

"Yes, Miss. Thank you."

When Felix discharged Allison at the front entrance of Wellington, John Farber and both Grayson's, Zachary and Matthew, had already been served drinks by a smartly uniformed Gretchen, and Martha had set up the dining room for buffet-style hors d'oeuvres.

"Welcome, gentlemen," Allison said as she entered hurriedly from the foyer where she had dropped her purse and coat on a chair. "I hope you haven't been waiting long."

"Just long enough to unwind a bit," Zach said, standing and lifting his glass. Matthew and John stood, as well.

"Please be seated," Allison said as she gestured toward the tastefully upholstered furniture.

Zachary Grayson's secretary was already seated, and Allison acknowledged her with a nod.

"Ms. Timmons."

"Hello, Ms. Harmon."

Gretchen was at Allison's side immediately, handing her a glass of her usual white wine. "Excuse me, Miss. The hor d'oeuvres can be served whenever you're ready."

"Thank you, Gretchen. Please tell Martha that we'll complete our business first. Oh, and Gretchen, tell Martha I'd like to speak with her later this evening."

"Yes, Miss."

"Well, then, shall we get started?" Allison asked, addressing her question to Zach.

"Yes, of course," Zach said. "As you know, the reading aloud of your father's will is a necessary formality. Ms. Timmons will serve as a witness, if that's all right with you. I assure you that she can be trusted with any confidences."

"Of course," Allison said, smiling at Ms. Timmons.

"If, at any time, you wish to stop the proceedings and ask a question, feel free," Matthew Grayson added.

Nearly an hour later, Zach closed the thick folder from which he had been reading and pronounced the procedure complete.

"As you can see, your father was quite detailed and specific in his bequests, Allison," Zach said.

"He certainly was," Allison said with a chuckle. "It doesn't surprise me in the least. I'm very pleased that he made provisions for our dedicated staff here at Wellington. I knew there was a trust fund, but I had no idea it was so substantial."

"Unlike your grandfather, your father was a very generous man," John said.

Allison had to hold back tears as she recalled specific instances of Marcus's bighearted nature. He was her hero. He had always been her hero, and he was gone.

Quickly regaining her composure, Allison uttered, more as a question than a statement, "So, it would seem that the estate is healthy, and I don't need to rush into selling any assets."

"Absolutely," Zach assured her. "You are a very wealthy woman who should never have to worry about finances. With your grandfather's shrewd business ventures and your father's wise investments, Harmon & Harmon could go under tomorrow and you'd still be financially secure."

"Before the end of the year," John added, "you'll need to review the philanthropic recipients and let me know if you wish them to remain the same. But that doesn't have to be decided tonight. You may increase or decrease the donations at any time and the adjusted amounts will go into effect in January."

"For the time being," Allison said, "I think it would be wise to make as few changes as possible. Do you all agree?"

A chorus of, "Yes, right, absolutely," resounded in harmony.

"Now, I don't know about you, but I'm starving," Allison declared as she rang a bell for Gretchen.

By the time the guests left it was past nine p.m. and Allison was exhausted. Martha appeared from the kitchen where she had been cleaning up from the evening's repast and found Allison slumped in a chair at the foot of the long dining table. She had kicked off her shoes and released her hair from its moorings.

"You wanted to see me, Miss Allison?"

"Yes, Martha, but it can wait until morning. I'm sure you're tired. By the way, the food was delicious. Thank you for such a marvelous buffet."

"It was my pleasure, as always, and Gretchen was a big help. Why don't you get comfortable, Miss. Felix took your bag to your room, and Gretchen can draw you a bath. I'll finish up in the kitchen and meet you in the upstairs sitting room. Shall I bring you a pot of herbal tea?"

"That would be perfect. Thank you, and bring a cup for yourself."

As Allison rose to leave, Martha added, "Miss Allison, is everything all right? I mean, the will and everything ... is that why you need to..."

"Oh, Martha," Allison interrupted, "I didn't mean to worry you. No, everything's fine. I just wanted to ask you some questions about... listen, I'll see you in about thirty minutes, okay?"

"Yes, Miss."

"And tell Gretchen I can draw my own bath. You'll spoil me yet."

CHAPTER 21

Chelsea Ludwick was only too happy to accept Jack's dinner invitation. She had been trying to attract his attention since their first week in Paris back in September. Why did he wait so long to approach her? Up till now, he barely even acknowledged her except to say "hi" in passing. She had nearly given up, thinking he must surely be gay.

Chelsea chose her most alluring black dress for the date—the one with the dipping neckline and short, sassy skirt. With only two weeks in which to snag this gorgeous man, she had no time to waste with subtlety, even if it meant freezing her ass off in the middle of winter. She remembered reading in a magazine that men generally preferred a non-fussy look in women, so she decided to wear her long, blonde hair down and added just a touch of mascara and lip gloss. After waiting four months for Jack to notice her, she wanted to look irresistible.

❧

Jack still hadn't accomplished any fine dining in Paris, so he checked out several restaurants on the Internet to be sure he chose one he could afford. They met in the lobby where he helped Chelsea with her coat and ushered her outside to a taxi.

"You look nice," Jack offered awkwardly once they are seated. Actually, he thought she looked a bit sleazy in that almost-dress and spike heels, but he couldn't think of anything else to say.

"So do you," Chelsea responded with a shiver.

"Are you cold?"

"A little, but I'll be fine once we get to the restaurant. Where are we going?"

"Chez Marie. I hope that's okay."

"I've never been there. Is it good?"

"I guess we'll find out together."

"So, have you finished your fellowship?" he asked, hoping the conversation would proceed more easily at dinner.

"Almost. Have you?"

"I sent my dissertation yesterday."

"Great," she said with strained enthusiasm.

At the restaurant, Jack thought about Allison and wondered what it would be like to have *her* sitting across from him instead of Chelsea. Whenever she talked, his mind wandered. He found it difficult to feign interest in this woman, not because she wasn't interesting and attractive, but because she wasn't Allison.

After a couple of drinks, Chelsea loosened up considerably and began chattering non-stop. Jack was relieved to find that he was barely expected to enter the conversation, except to nod or interject an occasional, "I see."

Jack didn't care to divulge anything about himself. To do so would encourage intimacy, and he discovered he had no desire to be intimate with Chelsea Ludwick. *This was a mistake,* he concluded over crème Brule.

Despite the romantic atmosphere of Chez Marie and the divine meal, Jack couldn't get into the date. He realized that—other than several months of sexual deprivation—he had no true chemistry with this woman. If he continued to see her, he would only be using her, and he didn't believe in using people. How ironic that he planned the date to help forget about Allison, but he wasn't able to think about anything or anyone else all evening.

As they exited the restaurant, Chelsea became increasingly physical, touching Jack's arm and leaning against him seductively. In the taxi, she sidled up to him and placed her hand on his thigh. Jack became aroused and grabbed her hand, holding it between his, ostensibly to warm it against the cold. She slipped her other hand inside his jacket and snuggled closely.

"It seems even colder than when we left the hostel," she said, shimmying into Jack's side and wrapping his arm around her. "On a night like this, a girl needs a strong man to keep her warm. Why did you wait so long to ask me out, Jack? I've had my eye on you for quite some time," she crooned suggestively, caressing his chest.

"Oh, you know, that dissertation has been all-consuming," he lied, grabbing her other hand. If she were any closer, she'd be sitting on his lap. He didn't want to hurt her feelings. After all, he's the one who started this descent into perdition.

"What's wrong, Jack?" Chelsea asked.

"Nothing, nothing at all," he said, pulling her hand away a bit too forcefully. "Your hands are cold, that's all," he laughed. "Here, let me warm them."

As they exited the taxi, Chelsea toppled off her shoes, forcing Jack to catch her in his arms. Leaning against him and giggling she asked, "My room or yours?"

Oh, great! Look what you've gotten yourself into, Jack. What a bad idea this was. Now what?

Jack managed to help Chelsea through the door and into the lobby. He led her to a love seat in the far corner, away from the TV where the usual group of students gathered. "Here, let's sit for a few minutes while you regain your balance," Jack said. "Listen," he added as gently as possible. "I need to apologize."

"Apologize? For what? I'm the one who can't hold her liquor. I shouldn't have had two drinks on an empty stomach."

"No, it's not that. You're a beautiful, smart, sexy girl—uh, woman—Chelsea, and you deserve the truth."

"Oh boy, here it comes," she said, straightening her posture and suddenly looking a bit more sober. "Maybe I don't want to hear the truth. Maybe I just want to have some fun after four months of working my butt off." She started to raise her voice, causing the other students to look in their direction. "Well, don't worry, Mr. Jack Sanderling. It's no skin off my nose." She stood precariously and shook her finger at Jack. "I'll save you the trouble of telling me the truth. I'll tell *you* the truth," she shouted. "You're boring, Mr. Jack Sanderling, and we didn't have anything going, anyway. So, don't you worry about Chelsea. I'll be just hunky dory." She turned and headed for the stairs. "Don't call me and I won't call you. That's the truth, Mr. Jack Sanderling," she shouted, waving her silver sequined clutch in the air. Halfway up the stairs, she turned to the group of dazed onlookers and declared, "...and to all a good night!"

Seconds later, an upstairs door slammed and Jack slumped into the cushions of the love seat. *You've done some dumb things in your pathetic life, Sanderling, but this is the dumbest. What were you thinking?*

CHAPTER 22

"Here's some nice, hot chamomile tea, Miss Allison," Martha said as she entered the upstairs sitting room, carrying a tray laden with Oma's familiar china tea set. Following a most welcome bath, Allison changed into her robe and slippers and sprawled on the chaise checking her phone for messages.

"Wonderful, Martha. Thank you. Here, let me do that. You must be tired after such a long day." Allison jumped up, took the tray from Martha, and nodded toward the sofa. "Please, sit down."

"I must admit, I'm a bit weary, Miss. Thanks."

Allison poured two cups of tea, handed one to Martha, and took her place on the sofa with one leg tucked under her so that she faced the older woman.

"Martha, you have been like a mother to me all these years. I don't know how I would have managed without you. My father certainly couldn't have raised a motherless girl without your help."

Martha, looking embarrassed, started to interrupt. "Miss All—"

"Wait, please let me finish," Allison continued. "I want you to know that Daddy made provisions for you in his will." Martha's gaze shifted from her teacup to Allison's face. "You have a home here at Wellington for as long as you choose to stay, and you'll continue to receive your full salary, with benefits, after you retire. Should you require special assistance in your later years, it will be provided and paid for by the trust fund Daddy set up for you."

"Oh, Miss… Oh, Miss Allison. I was afraid you were letting me go and now this. Oh, my!" Martha's eyes glistened and her hands started to shake so much that she set her cup and saucer on the coffee table to prevent them from tumbling to the floor.

"How can I ever thank you? How can I thank Mr. Harmon, God rest his soul."

Allison set her cup and saucer beside Martha's and took the woman's hands in hers. "It's a small gesture compared to what you've given this family, Martha," she said with sincerity. Martha started to recoil, but then relaxed into the guarded embrace, allowing Allison to hold her work-worn hands for a moment. Allison knew she had crossed a line that had been carefully drawn for almost thirty years, but she genuinely loved this woman. *Lines be damned! This isn't nineteenth century England, after all.*

"Martha, there *is* something you can help me with," Allison interjected in time to prevent Martha losing control of her emotions. Such a display, she sensed, would cause the proud woman unnecessary embarrassment.

"Of course, anything," Martha said, gently releasing her hands from Allison's clasp.

"I've been having these dreams lately. Well, not dreams, exactly, but flashes of memory. I need to ask you some questions about my childhood."

"Questions about what, exactly?" Martha said, now avoiding eye contact.

"I sense that my father tried to keep something from me—some kind of secret." Martha grew visibly tense. "Can you think of anything he didn't want me to know? Something he thought I was too young to understand?"

Martha stood and began to load the tea tray. "Some things are best left alone, Miss Allison."

"There *is* something! I knew it! You must tell me, Martha. I thought I was going crazy, that my imagination was... What is it?"

"I promised your father, Miss. I promised your grandfather. I didn't want to keep it from you. I thought you had a right to know, but they made me promise."

"They're both gone now, Martha, and I'm a grown woman. Whatever it is, I can handle the truth. What I can't handle is the not-knowing."

Martha paced and wrung her hands. "Oh, Miss Allison, I wanted you to know, but once it was done I hoped you'd never find out. Then, I nearly got up the nerve the night of your father's funeral, but I decided you'd had enough upset for one day."

Allison stood and moved toward the fireplace. Fleetingly, she noticed she was feeling especially tired, even achy tonight. Her eyes darted about the room as she tried to piece together the fragments of memory that continued to torment her.

Turning to face the visibly disturbed woman, her voice escalated. "Something happened when I was very young... something that everyone kept from me. I know that now." Allison grew more agitated and her head was pounding. "Was it about my mother? I remember her crying a lot. Please, Martha, I have to know."

"Oh, my God!" Martha said. "Your mother! I completely forgot until this moment. After my husband and... after I lost my family, I put it out of my mind and never... It was so long ago."

"Forgot what? What are you talking about?"

"Wait right here, Miss," Martha said rushing out the double door and down the corridor.

"Martha, come back. We're not finished," Allison called after her.

"I'll be right back." Martha's voice trailed off as she headed down the staircase to her private quarters, her shoes clicking at a faster pace than Allison had heard for many years.

Allison dropped into the nearest chair, wondering what just happened, and waited.

CHAPTER 23

When Martha returned a few minutes later, she was carrying a small brown envelope. Allison approached her gingerly. "What is it?" she asked.

"Please sit down, Miss. Your dear mother gave this to me just after she discovered she had terminal cancer. You were only five. She asked me to give it to you when you turned eighteen. Oh, Miss Allison, I'm so sorry! It was shortly after that when my husband and only child were taken from me in that terrible accident. Then I lost my home. I was in a sorry state back then."

"I can imagine. It must have been a terrible shock," Allison said.

"Anyway, I put the key away for safe keeping at the bottom of my blanket chest and never once thought about it again until a few minutes ago. It's the key to a safe deposit box at the bank."

"Which bank? My father has used many banks over the years."

"No, a different bank… in Brooklyn. Your mother didn't want your father to know about it. See? It's printed here on the outside."

Martha turned the envelope over so Allison could read the name: New York Trust Bank. "What's in it, Martha? What's in the box?"

"I don't know, Miss, but I think it will explain everything. Mrs. Harmon—your mother—never wanted to keep secrets from you, but your grandfather was a proud and stubborn man, and a powerful one. It wouldn't do to cross him."

Allison breathed deeply to settle her nerves a bit, and spoke calmly. "Martha, please tell me what you know."

"You're right. You're not a little girl anymore and you have the right to know everything. I should have told you years ago. I'll start from the beginning."

Allison moved back to the sofa and curled up in the corner, hugging her knees to her chest. Martha turned to face her, pain etched on her wrinkled face. As a child, Allie used to assume this very same position for her nightly bedtime stories. After Evelyn died, Marcus had suggested hiring a governess, but Martha insisted she could handle the added responsibility. She convinced him that since Allie was in school most of the day, and on the weekends she accompanied her father everywhere, it would be no trouble to look after her in the evenings.

"Before you were two years old, your mother had a baby," Martha began. Allison felt her eyes widen, but she allowed Martha to continue.

"The baby was born right here in the house. You see, it was hard for the Harmon family to enjoy any privacy, so she carefully kept her pregnancy hidden from anyone outside the immediate family. The doctor always came to Wellington for her check-ups. She was so happy. They both were."

"I remembered something about a baby, but I couldn't... What was it?" Allison asked.

"A boy," Martha answered sadly. "They named him Marcus, of course, Marcus Gregory Harmon the fourth."

"I had a brother? What happened to him?"

"He was so very beautiful and sweet-tempered... no trouble at all. For six weeks, your parents enjoyed him and you did, too. You loved to hold him and kiss him. Of course, you weren't old enough to realize he wasn't one of your dolls that you could push to the floor when you tired of holding him."

Allison leaned forward, a panicked look on her face. "Did I hurt him? I don't remember. I just can't remember."

"No, Miss, you didn't hurt him," Martha reassured her. "You were always well supervised."

"So, what happened?"

"Your parents planned a big party for Master Marc's two-month birthday. Your mother and grandmother addressed some two hundred invitations to be mailed the day after his six-week check-up. It was to be a grand catered affair with an orchestra and everything. Marcus Gregory Harmon the fourth would make his official entrance into the world just as you had at two months. The pediatrician came, as scheduled, to pronounce him healthy and robust, but that's not what happened."

"He was ill?" Allison asked.

"Worse. It was discovered that he was Mongoloid."

"Mongoloid? You mean he was mentally retarded?"

"That's what it was called back then. Now they call it Down syndrome."

"And? What happened?"

"Your parents were scarcely fazed by the news. They—especially your mother—had already bonded with their beautiful baby boy. They would love and nurture him right here at Wellington and hire whatever help was needed to give him as normal an upbringing as possible."

"How long did he live, Martha? My parents must have been devastated. No wonder I remember my mother crying so often. I always thought it was because of her cancer diagnosis. I must have been very young when he died."

"Miss Allison, he didn't die."

"What?" Allison asked incredulously. "What do you mean?" Allison stood with a jerk and started pacing and gesturing wildly. "Are you saying I have a brother, a living brother I haven't seen since I was two?"

"Yes, Miss," Martha answered, ashamedly.

"Where is he? What happened to him? Why wasn't I told? Why didn't Daddy tell me? How could he keep something like this from me? I'll never forgive him—never!"

"Listen to me, please. Come, sit down," Martha urged. "You can't blame your parents. You mustn't blame them. Let me explain."

Allison took a deep breath, trying to absorb this unbelievable revelation, and sat next to Martha. She held her aching head in her hands as Martha continued.

"As I said before, your grandfather was a powerful man and very obstinate. He had total control of the family at that time. In his youth, there was a ridiculous stigma about children with disabilities, and he decided the family and the business would be ruined if word got out about his grandson."

"Where is he, Martha?" Allison asked in a very weak voice, not only because she felt a cold coming on, but also because she felt like she had her world pulled out from under her.

"Your grandfather had him sent to an orphanage for 'special' children. I'm not sure, but I think it's in Utica."

"How could my parents let that happen? How could they let Opa send my brother...their son, away to a...a home...a home for orphans?" Allison was crying hysterically now.

"He wasn't an orphan. He had... he *has* a family."

Allison couldn't recall Martha ever hugging or even touching her, not even when Allison was a child. But now Martha put her arm around the young woman's shoulders and let Allison's tears mingle with her own.

"Oh, Allie, I'm so sorry. I should have told you."

"I hate him and Oma, too."

"He was a hard man, and so old-school," Martha continued. "There was no reasoning with him. Your grandmother tried, and it cost her a happy marriage. He was convinced that a 'defective' heir would ruin the family's reputation and the business that he had spent his entire life building. He told your father he would disinherit him and you, too, if he or your mother ever tried to see their son. Eventually, it was as if Marc had never been born. No one was allowed to mention him ever again. He swore the entire staff to secrecy and threatened to ruin any of us who challenged him or leaked the news to the press."

"Martha, that's terrible!"

"I'm so sorry, Miss Allison. I should have told you long ago, as soon as your grandfather died, but by the time you went to college it somehow seemed better to let things be. Please forgive me."

"It's not your fault. I have to find him. Do you remember the name of the home?"

"No. Only your grandfather knew."

"There must be a record somewhere. Maybe that's what's in the safe deposit box. I'll go to Brooklyn first thing tomorrow morning. Thank you for telling me the truth." Allison pulled a tissue from her pocket and blew her nose. "Now let's get some sleep. Tomorrow is going to be a big day."

Instead of sleeping soundly, Allison tossed and turned, thinking, planning, and trying to remember.

CHAPTER 24

Jack couldn't wait to board the plane and get home. He spent the last two weeks in Paris wandering from one museum to another, trying to avoid Chelsea Ludwick and trying unsuccessfully to forget Allison Harmon. *For someone who supposedly hasn't had time for a love life, I certainly have made a mess of mine.*

Fortunately, Chelsea stayed holed up in her room most of the time, frantically finishing her dissertation. When they did see each other at meals, she carefully avoided eye contact and pretended to have an in-depth and overly animated conversation with whomever was sitting next to her. Jack knew he owed her an apology for leading her on, but it was painfully obvious she would never be receptive enough to approach. *This relationship stuff is just too hard*, he decided. *Maybe I should find a monastery and be done with women for good.* The problem was that he couldn't stop thinking about Allie.

CHAPTER 25

Allison awoke with a start and a headache at eight o'clock Saturday morning. She had planned to get up at seven, but she must have inadvertently silenced the alarm and dozed off again. She needed coffee, strong coffee. Martha would have it waiting for her in the dining room, along with her sumptuous homemade cinnamon rolls. Martha always made cinnamon rolls when Allison spent the night at Wellington. They had been her favorite breakfast since childhood. In fact, serving this special delicacy was the only way Martha could ever get Allison to eat breakfast.

As Allison descended the staircase, she smelled the familiar, delicious aroma and followed it to the dining room, half expecting to see her father sitting in his arm chair at the head of the expansive table. *Oh, Daddy*, she thought, *how could you have kept my brother, my only sibling, from me? We could have been together all these years*. As she poured a cup of coffee from the pot on the sideboard, Gretchen entered from the kitchen, carrying a plate of warm cinnamon rolls.

"Good morning, Miss Harmon," she said. "Would you like eggs this morning?"

"No, thank you, but I'll take one of those." She nodded at the gooey mountain of dough dripping with butter, brown sugar, and cinnamon. "Yum, scrumptious as ever," she said, sinking her teeth into one.

"Will there be anything else, Miss?" Gretchen asked. Allison lifted her index finger signaling Gretchen to wait until she swallowed. "Yes," she finally answered. "Please ask Felix to have the car ready at nine o'clock. I'll be going to Brooklyn this morning, but first I need to make some calls."

"Will you need a bodyguard, Miss?"

"No, Felix will do."

"Yes, Miss."

Allison pulled her cell phone out of her robe pocket and did a quick Internet search for "New York Trust Bank, Brooklyn." She spent the next hour calling every single listing while dressing as quickly and warmly as possible.

At nine o'clock sharp Felix met her in the foyer, resembling an Eskimo.

"It's mighty cold outside this mornin', Miss Allison, and the weatherman's callin' for more snow," Felix announced as she descended the stairs. "I've got the car all warmed up for ya."

"Thanks, Felix. Here's the address. Well, at least I hope this is it." Her search identified twenty-four New York Trust banks in Brooklyn alone, and four of them claimed to have accounts under the name of Evelyn T. Harmon.

"All right, Miss. Let's be on our way, then. Watch those steps, now. They're a might slick with ice this mornin'."

Allison scarcely noticed the frigid air. Holding the precious envelope in her gloved hand, she felt her heart pumping blood through her Harmon veins—the same blood that flowed through the veins of her only brother. She *will* find him. They *will* be reunited. She'll deal with the anger and resentment later. Today there was room in her heart only for unbridled anticipation.

CHAPTER 26

Silvia Sanderling boarded the train to Washington, D.C. where she would spend a few days with Simon and Carolyn. One whole suitcase was filled with carefully selected gifts for them and for Jack. Her youngest son and his wife promised to take her to the National Cathedral for the Christmas Eve service and drive her through town to see the display of lights and decorations. Then, on the twenty-seventh she would be on her way to Penn Station where Jack would meet her. She hadn't seen either of her sons since June, and she felt like she would jump out of her skin with excitement.

Silvia had also hoped to see Zavie and meet his girlfriend—or rather his fiancée, Roberta—but Zavie and Roberta will be spending Christmas in Jamaica this year. Zavie hasn't been able to visit his family for six long years. However, since his recent commissioning to provide all of the artwork for Donald Trump's new hotel chain in the Caribbean, Zavie Johnson can afford to travel anywhere in the world. Won't his parents be proud of their son, the successful artist? Silvia couldn't be happier for him.

The train ride, though relaxing, seemed interminable. Although Silvia downloaded plenty of reading material to her IPad, she found it difficult to concentrate. *Must this train stop at every tiny town in Virginia,* she wondered.

The distinguished-looking bearded man occupying the adjacent seat noticed Silvia's restlessness. "Are you all right, Madam? You seem rather distressed," he said in a delightful British accent.

"Oh, I'm sorry. Am I bothering you?" Silvia asked.

"No, no, I just wondered if you needed any help. You seem to have lost something."

"I'm fine, thank you, just excited. I tend to get fidgety when I'm excited. I'm traveling to visit my sons whom I haven't seen in six months."

"I see. Where do your sons live, if you don't mind my inquiry?"

"I never tire of talking about my boys. Well, Jack—he's my eldest—lives in New York City…Manhattan. He just returned from Paris, and Simon—who's married—lives in Arlington."

"What about you?" she asked. "No, let me guess. You're a professor, right?"

"Is it that obvious?"

"Let's see, reading glasses, beard, brief case, suede shoes, corduroy blazer, British accent. I'm afraid you fit the stereotype to a tee," Silvia observed, studying him from head to toe.

"I didn't realize there *was* a stereotype," he said. "I must say you are spot-on, though. I teach at NYU."

"English Lit., right?" Silvia asked, confident of her assumption.

"Well, well, I do believe I've just met my first clairvoyant."

"Not at all," she said touching his book to reveal the cover. "It's just that, well, nobody reads Thomas Hardy for *pleasure*," she declared with a chuckle. Realizing he hadn't caught the humor in her

little joke, she quickly changed the subject. "So, what brings you to Virginia, Professor?"

"I was attending a conference in Roanoke. From your accent, I presume you are a native of the area?"

"Yes. I grew up in the western part of the state and have lived in Bedford since I got married almost thirty years ago. I'm a teacher, too—fourth grade."

"Ah, I have great respect for teachers of young children. I wouldn't have the patience, I'm afraid."

"I can't imagine doing anything else," Silvia said. "I love my work, and I love my students."

"So I see. It seems that we'll be traveling companions for a bit. Perhaps we should introduce ourselves. I'm Dr. Edward Hastings." He offered his hand and added, "But please, call me Edward."

"I'm pleased to meet you, Edward. I'm Silvia. Silvia Sanderling."

"Likewise, Mrs. Sanderling."

"Oh, it's Ms.," she hastened to add, wondering why she felt compelled to clarify that point. "I've been a widow for years, but please call me Silvia."

"Well, Silvia, it seems we have much in common. I, too, am widowed. I say, would you care to join me in the dining car for a cup of tea?"

"As long as I don't have to eat that wretched train food," Silvia said. "I brought along my sons' favorite homemade cookies. I'm sure they won't mind sharing." She pulled a Christmas tin from her satchel and preceded Edward through the swaying aisles toward the dining car.

CHAPTER 27

Allison trembled with both excitement and chills as Felix dropped her off at the first New York Trust Bank on her list.

"There isn't a parking place in sight, Miss. Will you be long?"

"It shouldn't take more than half an hour," she answered, pulling her collar up to her chin. The snow hitting her face felt more like ice, her throat hurt, and she was glad she didn't have far to walk.

"I'll circle the block until I see you out front, then."

Not ten minutes later Allison exited the building, disappointed but anxious to proceed to the next location.

Bank number two was located across from a parking garage where Felix could wait until she finished her business. If Felix wondered what his employer was up to, he didn't ask. Early in his career as a chauffeur, her father had taught him that the best way to ensure job security was to ask no personal questions of one's employer and to keep in strictest confidence all private conversations and observations.

This time Allison was gone a bit longer, but when she returned she carried two cups of coffee from Starbucks.

"Here, this should warm us up," she said, handing one cup to Felix.

"Oh, thank you, Miss. It'll hit the spot, for sure."

"Two creams, two sugars, right?" she asked.

"You remembered. Thank you."

As they sipped the hot, strong brew, Allison programmed into her GPS the address for the next bank on her list, determined not to let another dead end discourage her. She *will* find the safe deposit box, and she will *never* stop looking for her brother.

"The third time's the charm." Allison mumbled more to herself than to Felix.

"Miss?"

"The next bank is only two blocks away," she said, clearing her scratchy throat. "I can walk from here."

"It's getting mighty nasty out there, Miss Allison. The sidewalks'll be slippery. I'll come with you."

"I'll be fine, Felix."

"I'd feel better, Miss Allison."

"Oh, all right. Let's go, then," she said, clearing her throat that had advanced from sore to raging.

Heavy sleet was falling and the brisk wind made it feel even icier. Although they dressed warmly, the unexpected icy rain soaked through Allison's wool coat.

"We should've brought an umbrella," Felix nearly shouted to be heard over the combination of traffic noise and pelting sleet.

"You can say that again," Allison shouted into her coat lapel. She pulled her scarf tightly about her neck and held it there with one hand as she held fast to Felix's arm with the other.

Finally, they arrived at the bank and rushed inside, dripping wet and shivering.

"I'll wait here by the radiator," Felix said. "Don't be long, Miss. You're soaking wet."

Sometimes Felix acts more like a parent than an employee, Allison thought. *I should be annoyed, but it's actually kind of sweet,* she decided.

Allison approached a teller and tried to speak, but her voice wouldn't cooperate. She cleared her scratchy throat and managed to croak her request.

A minute or two later, the teller ushered her to a vault in the rear of the bank filled from floor to ceiling with safe deposit boxes. The teller climbed a ladder to reach door number 323, inserted a key, and pulled out the box. *Could this really be it?* Allison wondered as the woman lowered the box from its perch. Next, Allison was led to a small cubicle where she could open the box in private.

"Here you go, Ma'am. Just let me know when you've finished."

"Thank you," Allison said in a cracking voice. At this point, her throat was on fire and her head was pounding. She shook both from excitement and the onset of a fever as she removed her key from its envelope marked with the number 323 and tried to insert it in the lock. What would she find? What did her mother place in the box all those years ago? Would this small metal strong box hold the answers to her questions and shed light on those crazy, fragmented memories? More importantly, would it reveal her brother's whereabouts?

Using one hand to steady the other, she finally managed to insert the key and turn the lock. To her utter amazement, the lid opened. She pulled out the contents and placed them on the table. Inside, she found a large manila envelope labeled, "Allie." *Can this really be happening?* she wondered. *After all these years, can my mother actually be reaching out to me from her grave?*

Not here, Allison thought through the haze of her mounting fever. *I must get home before I open it.* She shoved the envelope into her purse and began to put her gloves back on. Standing to leave, she realized the room had grown very hot and her head was spinning. She needed air. She needed to get home, but right now, she felt like she could barely put one foot in front of the other. *What's happening to me?* Managing to make it back to the lobby, she tried to signal Felix to come to her aid, but she was too weak and dizzy. Then, everything went black and, before Felix could reach her, she sank to the floor.

CHAPTER 28

Allison, under the guise of Rebecca Jones, awoke in a hospital room in Brooklyn, feeling like she had run a marathon. A nurse was taking her pulse. Every muscle in her body ached and she was too weak to speak or even hold her eyes open.

"Welcome back, dear," the nurse said in a cheerful voice.

Allison had no idea where she was coming back from, but staying awake required too much effort, she decided. She closed her heavy eyelids and, once again, sank into a tunnel of darkness where dreams awaited.

Her father is there and her mother, too, but they are young. Mommy is holding a tiny bundle. Opa is pushing Mommy along a cavernous hallway with closed doors on either side. Mommy turns back to look at Daddy with pleading, tear-filled eyes. Daddy's outstretched arms try to reach her, but his feet do not budge.

Before she closed her eyes, she heard a television news anchor reporting, "Billionaire executive, Allison Harmon, collapses in lobby of Brooklyn bank."

CHAPTER 29

Jack Sanderling's airplane landed at LaGuardia two weeks before Christmas. With his dissertation defense only days away, he must recover quickly from jetlag, scurry to prepare the apartment for his mother's arrival, and do some last-minute shopping. Although Silvia will spend a few days, including Christmas day, with Simon and Carolyn, Jack wanted to put up a tree and decorate a bit for her arrival on the twenty-seventh. He had been able to order tickets to "Phantom" online, so at least that was done. He also managed to send gifts to Simon and Carolyn with the help of the Internet. He and Zavie agreed to wait to exchange gifts until Zavie and Roberta returned from Jamaica in January when, together, they can enjoy a combination Christmas/engagement/graduation celebration.

Outside the airport, Jack splurged on a taxi. With so much baggage, he couldn't imagine trying to maneuver his way on and off the crowded subway. Finally, standing in front of his apartment building, he prepared to haul two heavy suitcases, plus a duffle bag, backpack, and computer bag up four flights—a two-trip chore which he intended to follow with a hot shower and a long nap.

On the first trip, Jack opened the door just wide enough to set the suitcases inside, not bothering to switch on the light before heading back downstairs. Finally, the arduous task was finished, and when Jack turned on the light, to his amazement, he was greeted with a spotless apartment and a beautifully decorated Christmas tree. Above the front windows a huge banner spanned the entire width of the wall. It read, "Welcome home, Dr. Sanderling! Merry Christmas! Love, Zavie and Roberta." Jack couldn't believe his eyes. Glancing about the apartment, he noticed other festive touches, such as candles and wreathes, garlands and poinsettias. *What a great guy*, he thought, collapsing to the floor in happy exhaustion. Sprawled on the area rug—to catch his breath for just a minute—he fell into a deep sleep.

Nearly two hours later, Jack awoke with a start. At five p.m. both the Christmas tree lights and the window candles switched on automatically and woke him. *Zavie thought of everything*. His back felt stiff from lying on the floor. Rolling to his stomach, Jack did a few cat stretches and decided to order a pizza. He wished Zavie were there to share it with him. Unpacking and laundry could wait until tomorrow, but he knew he had to stay awake until at least midnight or he'd have a hard time recovering from jetlag.

While he waited for the pizza delivery, Jack turned up the thermostat and took a shower. Then, hoping to find just one beer in the fridge, he discovered that Zavie stocked it with a whole carton of beer, plus all manner of food. There were packages of sandwich meat, bagels, several kinds of cheese, fresh vegetables, yogurt, a gorgeous carrot cake, and who-knew-what else behind all of that bounty. *Wait till I see that roommate of mine. I'm going to give him a huge bear hug.*

Finally, Jack settled in for a night of pepperoni pizza, beer, and mindless TV. Determined to stay awake, he got up and performed jumping jacks or push-ups whenever drowsiness threatened to overtake him. Channel-surfing resulted in one Christmas special after another, but finally he landed on a showing of *Saving Private Ryan*. *If that movie doesn't keep me awake, nothing can,* he thought.

During the commercials, Jack sent text messages to Zavie, filling him in on the details of his trip home and thanking him for his thoughtfulness.

"Got home around three. Awesome surprise, Buddy! Thanks!"

"It was fun. Glad you like it."

"Great decorations. Mom will love them."

"Roberta's touch. Keep it clean or answer to her."

"Can't wait to meet her."

"She's amazing. Sorry to miss your Mom. Hugs from me."

"Will do. Thanks again. Will call Christmas day."

Jack managed to stay up until the eleven o'clock news came on. Deciding to "hit the hay" as soon as it finished, he made sure the bed was ready and waiting. While listening to the world news segment, he pulled down the Murphy bed, threw on some clean sheets and a blanket, and added two pillows from the closet. Then, he carried the nearly empty pizza box to the kitchenette and began to wrap the leftover pieces in aluminum foil. The newscaster's next words caused him to freeze, holding a slice of pizza in mid-air.

"In local news, corporate president Allison Harmon remains hospitalized, recovering from pneumonia. Last week, Ms. Harmon collapsed in the lobby of a New York Trust bank and was rushed by ambulance to an undisclosed hospital in Brooklyn. Our sources say that her condition is serious, and she is expected to remain hospitalized until the New Year."

Immediately, all bitterness toward Allison drained from Jack's mind. He just wanted to hold her and make her feel better. Every miserable moment spent thinking about her turned into a yearning to be with her, to tell her how he felt about her. Resentment became resolve. *I have to find her. God knows I've tried to forget her, but I can't. How will I ever stop this crazy roller coaster unless I confront her and talk about what happened? Maybe there's a logical explanation. But first I have to make sure she's okay. Tomorrow, I'll find her tomorrow.*

He turned off the TV, climbed into bed, and tried to sleep, but he could only think about Allison. Alone in the dark, Jack's mood vacillated from anxiety to melancholy and back again. *What if it's too late? What if she found someone else? What if she dies before I can tell her I'm sorry... that I want a chance with her?* His mind was racing, wavering between reality and imagination. *But who is it I think I love? Allison Harmon, the president of a major corporation? Allison Harmon, the billionaire? No, it's Allie, the beautiful, uncomplicated girl I met in a Paris park. But which is the real Allison? Is it possible that both are real? I have to find out, even if it means getting my heart stomped again. Obviously, I can't move forward until I know for sure.* Finally, Jack drifted off to sleep, but he woke on Paris time and decided to go for a run.

CHAPTER 30

Allison sat up for the first time in days. She felt weaker than a baby kitten, but glad to see Theo standing in the doorway. Every time she tried to talk, she had a violent coughing spell, but she wanted—needed—to find out what was going on at work.

"Well, don't you look, uh, just, well, dreadful," Theo said. She could tell he came fully prepared to cheer her with jokes and rehearsed compliments, but evidently her shocking appearance made it difficult to maintain a light-hearted mood.

"Gee, thanks," she responded in a bass voice that barely resembled hers.

Regaining composure, Theo quickly said, "Oh, it's nothing that a little TLC won't cure... and maybe a bottle or two of shampoo."

"I know, I must look a fright," she agreed, running her hand weakly through her stringy, matted hair. "Don't forget, I've been dying here." A sudden coughing spell wracked her body until she thought she might actually vomit. Theo handed her the water cup from her tray and she took a few sips through the straw. Exhausted, she flopped back on the pillow and closed her eyes.

"The nurses tell me you've been here every day," Allison whispered, her eyes still closed. "Thanks, Theo. Are all these flowers and balloons from you?"

"This is only a fraction of them. We left at least this many at the office and Felix says that many arrangements have arrived at Wellington, too. They're from all over the world."

"Really? How very thoughtful and kind." She started to cry, but was once again overcome by gut-wrenching coughs.

"Hey, I'd better not stay long. You need to rest," Theo said, genuine concern etched on his brow.

"I've rested enough for a lifetime," she said, rubbing her aching chest. "How long have I been here?"

"You were in Intensive Care for three days. Altogether, you've been here for six days."

"Did I miss Christmas?"

"Tomorrow is Christmas Eve," Theo said, as Allison's breathing grew more labored.

"Should I call a nurse?"

"Yes, but don't go yet, okay?" she wheezed.

"Okay, but don't try to talk anymore. I'll be back in a few minutes."

Allison was only too happy to oblige since talking wore her out and made her cough uncontrollably. Minutes later, a nurse arrived to give her a breathing treatment and administer a hypodermic while Theo went to the cafeteria for a cup of coffee.

When Theo returned with a cup for Allison, she was breathing easier and felt like there was a little more color in her cheeks.

"Thank you," she said feebly, taking the coffee from him. "It isn't Starbucks, but it'll do. Listen, Theo. I need your help with something."

"Of course," he replied.

"Where are the clothes I was wearing when I arrived?"

"I don't know. Why? You're not leaving here anytime soon, you know."

"I know, but I need my bag. I put something in it that I need. Can you find it, please?"

"Of course. They probably locked it up for safe-keeping. I'll check at the nurse's station."

"Wait, Theo. I want to tell you something before the medication makes me sleepy."

"Okay, what is it?" She was starting to get agitated again, and she knew Theo recognized that. "You shouldn't get upset. How about tomorrow? I'll be back tomorrow."

"No, I'm not upset, I'm excited, thrilled, actually, but I need your help," Allison assured him. "It's a long story, but Theo, I have a brother."

"A brother?" Theo asked, sounding incredulous. "How do you know? Where is he?"

"That's just it. I don't know where he is, but I have to find him. Will you help me?" Allison pleaded.

"Yes, of course, but how?"

"Find my bag, and I'll tell you everything."

When Theo returned minutes later, Allison was drifting into sleep. He lifted her arm gently and, pulling the covers up, laid the satchel underneath. *After twenty-five years of not knowing about the existence of a sibling, tomorrow will be soon enough,* she thought.

CHAPTER 31

The morning of December twenty-fourth brought group after group of carolers to the hospital, but Allison was not interested in listening to them. She was not interested in breakfast, either, but a tray was brought anyway. She took a couple of sips of coffee and drank the juice, then pushed the tray aside. Determined to never again celebrate a Christmas without her brother, she opened her bag and prepared to unseal the envelope that she hoped would divulge his whereabouts. She lifted a prayer of supplication that this would be a momentous day—a life-changing day—for both of them. Carefully, tentatively, she opened the envelope, spilling the contents onto her blanket. Inside she found a smaller envelope and photographs, nearly a dozen of them, and a pair of blue baby booties that appeared to have been hand-knitted.

One picture showed her parents with a little girl who surely must be she. She had forgotten how beautiful her mother was. Allison was sitting on her young-looking father's lap, and her mother was holding a tiny baby. They all looked so happy, a perfect happy family! "Marc," she exclaimed. "My baby brother, Marc."

The next picture showed her holding her little brother. Reaching from behind her, someone's hand was visible helping her support the baby's head. She was gazing adoringly upon his sweet, sleeping face. The tears began to flow, and they continued as she leafed through the remaining photographs: Allie, no more than a baby herself, was bending down to kiss Marc on the forehead; Marcus was holding his son, proudly displaying him for all the world to see; there was another picture of the four of them and one of Allie wearing a T-shirt that said, "I'm the Big Sister." *How could they have let him go? Why didn't they fight harder? How could Opa have been so heartless?*

Feeling both excitement and trepidation, she unsealed the smaller envelope. It was a letter, handwritten by her mother. The paper had yellowed from age and the ink was a bit faded, but it was a treasure that Allison would safeguard for the remainder of her life, whether or not it answered her questions and revealed the truth about her family's secret. It was the only communication from her mother in her mother's words, touched by her mother's hand and kept safely locked away through her mother's will. It was a treasure, indeed!

Slowly, carefully, Allison unfolded the stationery, four pages thick, and began to read:

My Darling Allie,

If you are reading this, you are old enough to know the truth. I'm so sorry I have to leave you, especially at such a young age. I love you very much, and more than anything, I want to watch you grow up and share the privilege of celebrating every milestone along the way. I want to be there for every birthday. I want to prepare you to enter womanhood and watch you go on your first date. I want to be there for your high school graduation and visit you at college. I want to help you plan your wedding and to meet my grandchildren. But it's not to be. I'm told that I have only a few months to live.

Of course, I know that you will someday take over the family business. Even at five, you talk of nothing else. But I hope you will also find purpose outside of your career and that you will find love, as I have. I have loved your father, and I have loved you with all my heart. My darling girl, I've learned that love, when given away, only multiplies. It can be split a million times over and never diminish.

There is someone else who has possessed my heart without diminishing my love for you. You were never supposed to know, but I couldn't let you live your entire life as a lie the way I've had to these past four years. You have a right to know that you are a sister. That's right, my Allie. You have a brother. He was born when you were only twenty months old, so I feel certain you don't remember him. I pray that somehow, someday you and he might be reunited.

I'm so ashamed that I didn't fight harder to keep him, and now it's too late. His name is Marc, by the way, Marcus Gregory IV. It grieves me that he is named after his cruel, heartless grandfather. You see, your Opa took him from us and sent him away. We found out that Marc is mentally disabled, and your grandfather is ashamed to have an imperfect grandson carry his name and his legacy into the future.

I hope someday you can forgive your daddy and me. We didn't want to give up our son. We begged and pleaded, but our baby boy was stolen away in the middle of the night without a single "good-bye."

Your grandfather was unmoved by our pleas. We felt like we had no choice, no influence, and now it's too late. I've tried to find him, Allie, but I'm pretty sure Opa changed his name so we couldn't track him down. Please look for him, Allie. Find your brother and tell him how much I love him and how sorry I am about everything.

Last year, I hired a private detective who found a possible link to a home for "special" orphans located just south of Utica. It's called "The Caring Cottage."

Of course, with your Opa's connections, he was able to have the records sealed, so I was never successful in my search. I drove there myself, only to find half a dozen boys fitting the age and description of your brother. After nearly four years, I simply couldn't be sure without a DNA test. I tried to hire an attorney to have the records opened, but your grandfather found out and threatened to ruin your father and prevent you from inheriting the business. Both of you would have been left with nothing. I'm not sure, but I think the monster had Marc transferred to another home after that. Then I got sick and unable to pursue it any further. I will go to my grave with this horrible, unrevealed secret on my conscience and a huge hole in my heart, but you don't have to.

Allie, now that you are eighteen—I'll bet you are a beautiful, smart young woman—you may have some legal rights. If you want to meet your brother as much as I want you to, don't give up trying to find him. Chances are, your grandfather is dead, and you and your father can pick up the search where I left off. There has to be a way to find him, and I feel sure that money is no object.

Please forgive me and forgive your daddy. Opa is a tyrant and your father fears him with good reason. Your daddy is a good man who is determined never to be like his father. He loves us, Allie, and he doesn't want either of us to suffer. He honestly believes that by shielding you from the truth, he is protecting you from a life of pain.

Please tell Marc that I always loved him and wanted him. I love you, too, my precious Allie Cat. I'll be looking down from heaven, watching you grow up and holding you in my heart forever until we meet again.

Your Mommy,

Evelyn Harmon

CHAPTER 32

When Jack finally reached room 556 at New York Community Hospital of Brooklyn, he found Allison crying hysterically and coughing ferociously. She looked like a prisoner of war who had just been released: thin, with sunken cheeks and dark-rimmed eyes. For a fleeting moment, he wasn't actually sure this pitiful-looking creature was his Allie. Risking the keen possibility of rejection, he rushed to her bedside, scooped her into his arms, and began rocking her back and forth.

"Jack?" she sniffled. "Is it really you? Oh, Jack, where were you? Why didn't you come? I thought…"

"Never mind. Just let me hold you. Allie, I missed you," he whispered into her filthy hair. "Are you all right?"

"I am now," she replied, much to his relief. "How did you find me?"

"It wasn't easy, Rebecca Jones. I heard about you on the news and went to your office. At first your assistant didn't believe me. He thought I was some crazy stalker, but then I told him the whole story about our meeting in Paris. He remembered your note about going to find a quiet park and how you were almost late for a meeting that afternoon. Finally, the details all started to fall into place. I'm pretty sure he did an Internet search on me, too."

They were both talking at once, each trying to explain to the other.

Jack said, "That's why you didn't tell me who you really were. I understand now."

"I would've told you everything the next day, but..."

"You were avoiding the press. I understand."

"I was going to tell you... but you didn't come," Allie said.

"I'm sorry. I thought you were toying with me."

"Of course, you did—I'm so sorry," Allie said. "I should've... Oh, dear, I must look ghastly."

"You look beautiful."

Jack handed her a tissue from the bedside table. "A little snotty, but beautiful," he added, causing her to laugh amidst her sobs. "Wow! Look at all these flowers," he exclaimed, glancing about the room. Then, suddenly remembering something, he pushed her away to reveal a dozen red roses crushed between them.

"Oh, Jack, thank you! Don't ever leave me again, okay?"

"I promise."

They embraced again and Jack spent the entire day at the hospital. The conversation picked up where it left off in Paris. She told him the whole truth about her identity, about H & H, and her responsibility to the firm. She talked about her father and Wellington Manor. Then, she told him about Marc and let him read the letter from her mother. He promised to help her find her brother. She promised to get out of the hospital in time for his hooding ceremony.

While Jack went to the cafeteria to grab a sandwich, Allie took her first shower in more than a week. The effort must have left her exhausted. When he returned to her room, Jack found her sprawled on top of the covers, wearing a soaked hospital gown. Evidently, she lacked the strength to towel herself dry. He tried not to think about the clear outline of her naked form revealed through the thin gown. Instead, he wrapped her in the hospital-issued robe a nurse had left for her, helped her under the covers, and gently combed the tangles from her hair.

As dusk fell, Allie mentioned that she hadn't seen Theo all day. "I wonder why Theo hasn't come today."

"Well, maybe it's because I convinced him to let me have you all to myself," Jack replied, looking a bit sheepish.

"How did you convince Theo that you weren't an ax murderer… or worse yet, paparazzi?"

"Like I said, it wasn't easy. He's very protective of you."

"I know. He's a good friend and a loyal employee."

A nurse walked in. "Miss Jones needs to get some rest now, young man. You're welcome to come back tomorrow."

"First thing tomorrow—It's Christmas!" he announced, jumping up. "The best Christmas ever!" Suddenly, Jack took the nurse in his arms and began waltzing about the room with her and singing "We Wish You a Merry Christmas." At first, she appeared startled, but when Allie started to giggle she relaxed into his arms and participated willingly in the revelry. Soon, however, Allie's laughter dissolved into another violent coughing spell and Jack's merriment quickly turned to concern.

"Is she okay?" he asked the nurse who rushed to her patient's aid. "I'm sorry, Al—I mean, Rebecca. Oh, God, you sound terrible!"

"She's fine," the nurse reassured him. "Her congestion is loosening up. It's a good sign, but you'd better go. She's had enough excitement for today."

"Okay, I'll be back in the morning," he promised, backing out of the room, afraid that if he took his eyes off her, Allie would disappear. Wracked with coughing, she somehow managed to blow him a kiss. He waited outside the door until her coughs subsided, then, passing the elevator, flew down five flights of stairs, missing half of the steps along the way. He felt like he could keep flying all the way home. For the first time in his life, Jack Sanderling was in love.

CHAPTER 33

Love seemed to be in the air during Christmas, or in Silvia's case, attraction at least. She had always thought of train travel as romantic, perhaps because of its long history, spanning centuries, actually. Movies certainly contributed to the romanticizing of what was intended as a basic mode of transportation: "From Russia with Love," "Love in the Afternoon," and "North by Northwest" to name a few. Who knew if this trip might generate actual romance? But Silvia was enjoying her traveling companion, nonetheless.

By the time Silvia and Edward finished drinking a whole pot of tea, they had become quite well acquainted. Silvia learned that Edward has a daughter, Katherine, who still lived in Bristol. She was married with two children. He visited her and her family each summer. Edward loved teaching at NYU, where he has worked for the last fifteen years, and he had no intention of returning to England to live. He told Silvia that his wife died of cancer when Katherine was twelve, and that raising a teenaged girl alone was an extremely challenging task. Silvia, who could relate to the trials of single parenthood, described her experience raising two rambunctious boys alone. They shared photographs of each other's children and—in his case—grandchildren. They exchanged stories about their respective careers as educators and discussed their plans for the holidays.

The easy conversation continued after they returned to their seats in Business Class and, by the time they reached Culpeper, it felt like they were the only two passengers on the train. Silvia found herself wishing they didn't have to go their separate ways in D.C. Evidently, Edward shared her reluctance to part. When the conductor announced, "Next stop, Union Station," the professor pulled a business card out of his wallet and invited Silvia to look him up when she reached New York.

"I will," she promised, "and if you're ever in Virginia again… well, here are my numbers." Silvia hurriedly scrawled both her home number and her cell phone number on a scrap of paper.

When she stood to depart, Edward gave her a gentle kiss on the cheek that felt ever so natural.

"It has been lovely talking with you, Silvia," he said.

"You too, Edward. Thank you for making a potentially boring trip very pleasant."

She hugged him in return. His well-groomed beard was soft and comforting, not bristly as she had expected. Helping her with her coat, he steadied her against the lurching movement of the car. Suddenly, she was in his arms and he kissed her on the lips. Surprising herself, Silvia felt no urge to push him away, this man who only a few hours earlier was a complete stranger. The kiss was tender and electrifying at the same time, and she wanted it to last longer.

"I'll see you in New York," she said, now feeling a bit embarrassed by her eagerness in returning his kiss.

"Do you promise?" he asked, tipping her chin up to look directly into her blue eyes.

"Absolutely. Goodbye, Edward, and Merry Christmas!"

"Merry Christmas, my Dear. I'll see you soon," he called after her. As she departed, she longed with every fiber of her being that he would follow her down the steps and onto the platform.

CHAPTER 34

Christmas day at New York Community Hospital began quietly. Any patients deemed even marginally well enough to go home had been released and the nursing staff was reduced to half its normal ranks. Allison awoke feeling much improved physically, but a little sorry for herself at having to remain there through the holidays. Yet, if she were to be released, where would she go and with whom would she celebrate? She hadn't accomplished the first bit of shopping, not even for the staff at Wellington, and she completely forgot to instruct Clarence to put up a tree at the Manor. Fortunately, Theo thought to direct Delores in payroll to take care of the annual employee bonuses at H & H, and the usual staff party was well in hand before Allison fell ill. Today her employees would be home with their families where they belonged. Despite anticipation of Jack's return, she couldn't help feeling a bit lonely and sad on her first Christmas without her father.

Shortly before eight a.m., the pulmonologist arrived to examine Allison, and to her astonishment announced that she should be able to go home in a couple of days. A few minutes later, while a nurse was helping Allie with her breathing treatment, Theo and James showed up laden with packages.

"What have you done?" she tried to say through the breathing tube.

"Since you can't go home for Christmas, we brought a little Christmas to you," Theo announced, depositing his load in the room's only chair.

Pulling the mouthpiece out so she could talk, Allison argued, "You should be with your families today."

"You're not the boss today, Miss Har... uh, Miss Jones. Now, put that thing back in your mouth and cooperate with this poor, overworked angel of mercy while we complete our mission."

Theo began opening an array of bags and boxes and decorating Allison's room with garlands of artificial greenery and red velvet bows. Left with no choice but to comply, she threw her hands in the air and plopped back on the pillows.

James's second trip to the car produced a fully decorated, miniature Christmas tree and two huge shopping bags filled with wrapped gifts. Theo flitted about the room, removing wilted flowers from the multitude of get-well arrangements and tidying every surface. "Now, we'll need this space for the buffet table. Let's set the tree over there where there's room to place the gifts underneath." He sounded like a movie director preparing his next scene.

"I don't believe this," Allison said once her treatment was finished. "Nurse Mandy, I promise I had nothing to do with this insanity."

"I know," Mandy said, looking like the proverbial cat that swallowed a canary. "Now, don't get too excited or I'll have to ask your friends to leave."

"Christmas lunch will be served at twelve on the dot," Theo declared to the nurse. "And everyone on the floor is invited: doctors, nurses, orderlies, and any patients who are able, okay?"

"I'll see to it, Mr. Rutledge," answered the nurse, observing, with satisfaction, Allison's wide eyes and dropped jaw.

"Wait a minute! I smell a conspiracy here," Allison said.

"Take your pill, Ms. Jones, and then it's nap time for you," instructed Mandy.

"Nap time! I couldn't possibly... oh, all right, I give up."

As Theo and James busily completed their tasks, they chatted back and forth like a couple of magpies. Allison watched in amazement, feeling as if she were an invisible observer. Finally, they turned their attention to her.

"Now, what can we do with this dreary part of the room?" Theo said, making sweeping motions in Allison's direction.

"I have a few ideas," James responded. "First, we start with wardrobe." Out of a Saks Fifth Avenue bag, he pulled a stunning red silk peignoir. "Off with zee rags!" he ordered in his best Pepé le Pew accent.

"Right here?" Allison asked, tightly grasping her hospital gown.

"My dear Mademoiselle, we gay men are unmoved by zee female physique," —which he pronounced 'veezeeque'—"but if you insist upon privacy, you shall have privacy." With that, James ceremoniously lifted the bed covers to create a modesty screen and turned his head in the opposite direction. When Allison tossed her hospital gown over the barrier, James gingerly took it between his thumb and index finger, declaring, "Zees, we must burn!"

Once Allison recovered from her initial shock, she began to relax and enjoy the comedy routine unfolding before her. Theo disappeared from the room, but Allison could hear him issuing orders to someone in the corridor.

"Now for zee hair and make-up," James announced flamboyantly. "Turn around, please Mademoiselle. James must undertake zee rats' nest." She complied with a giggle, and James deftly swept her hair into a loose chignon, leaving a few tendrils to frame her face. "Hope springs eternal! Let us zee what can be done with zee urchin's face."

A hair stylist and make-up artist by trade, James pulled his cosmetics case from a shopping bag, and with only a few brush strokes, erased nearly all traces of illness from his subject's face.

"Monsieur James, you are a miracle worker," Allison said, checking her reflection in the hand mirror that he provided.

Theo entered, followed by two orderlies carrying tables and chairs.

"Now, Mademoiselle, you must rest or I'll be in big trouble with Nurse Ratched," James said.

"Hey! Don't malign my wonderful nurse, or you shall be banned from my party. It is a party, isn't it?" Allison asked.

"Yes, but only if the hostess is well rested," Theo answered, pushing Allison back onto the pillows. "Now, do as you're told and close your eyes."

"Okay, okay, I do feel tired, but wake me when Jack comes. Promise?"

"I promise," Theo acquiesced, drawing the curtain around her bed. Then he proceeded to close the draperies and turn out the lights.

Around eleven thirty, Allison awoke to the smell of roasted turkey, accompanied by every other delicious aroma that one might associate with Christmas dinner. Sitting in the arm chair beside her bed was none other than Jack Sanderling, wearing a Santa hat.

"Theo promised to wake me when you arrived," Allison said, stretching and yawning. "How long have you been sitting there, Santa?"

"Only a few minutes. I couldn't bear to wake you. I must say, you look much better than you did yesterday."

"You said I looked beautiful, as I recall," she teased.

"Right. Well, today you look *stunningly* beautiful. I hope you're hungry." Jack stood and moved to Allison's side.

"I'm starved," she said as he embraced and fervently kissed her.

CHAPTER 35

A few minutes before noon, a commotion erupted beyond the curtain surrounding Allison's bed. Theo and James swooped into her room, followed by a parade of white-coated catering employees carrying sumptuous smelling trays of food. When Theo opened the curtain, he and a room full of hospital personnel announced, "Merry Christmas!"

At first Allison assumed she must be dreaming. The scene before her could not possibly be real, could it? But it was. Her hospital room had been transformed into a Christmas paradise. Two long tables, artfully decorated with red tablecloths, votive candles, and small poinsettias were set with Christmas china, sparkling crystal, and real silver utensils. Half a dozen patients in wheel chairs had been pushed in and were positioned around the tables. Behind them, several nurses, doctors, and orderlies lined the walls. Finally, when it seemed that the room couldn't possibly hold more bodies, Martha, Felix, and Allison's only cousins, Lydia and Lynette, entered with their husbands. She could hardly believe her eyes.

At first, Allison was speechless. Then, when she opened her mouth, she could only speak monosyllabic sounds. "Wha ... How? Oh! Wow!"

"That was an eloquent speech, Miss Jones," Theo teased. "Now, can we eat?" His comments were followed by a mixture of laughter and applause.

"Wait!" Allison exclaimed, coughing. Jack rushed to her side. "Please," she choked, raising her hand to signal "hang on." "I want to say thank you to, well, to everyone here, but especially to Theo and James… and Jack… for making this a wonderful Christmas, the most wonderful Christmas ever."

"Okay, folks, dig in," Theo interrupted.

"No, wait! I also want to say thanks to God, if I may. After all, it's *His* son's birthday, not mine." As everyone bowed their heads in prayer, Allison offered a simple but heartfelt prayer of thanks for good friends, good food, and excellent medical care. Then, struggling to contain the tears that threatened to surface, she climbed out of bed and, steadying herself on the comforting arm of Jack Sanderling, circulated among the guests, expressing her genuine gratitude for their attendance.

The nurses and doctors were served first so they could return to their duties, but not before each was presented a gift. "Theo, you thought of everything. How can I ever thank you? It's a perfectly marvelous party—but it must have cost a fortune!"

"Don't worry, boss. You're paying for it."

"I see," she said, wrinkling her forehead like a teacher who has just heard a confession from the instigator of a classroom brawl. "Well then, I had better hurry back to work while there's still a company to go back to."

They spent a delightful afternoon of eating, drinking champagne, and singing Christmas carols. Allison enjoyed introducing Jack to her cousins and employees, all of whom deduced that they'll being seeing a lot more of him in the future. Allison also shocked her cousins with the news about Marc. She shared the photographs from her mother and promised to keep them informed of any further developments. Martha was permitted access to the letter and pictures, but not until after the others departed. As Allison anticipated, it was an emotional moment for her housekeeper when Martha laid eyes upon the child who was stolen all those years ago, as much from her as from Allison and her parents.

"I *will* find him, Martha," Allison said as the woman wept silently into a handkerchief. Allison could not remember a time when Martha didn't have a clean, white handkerchief tucked inside the sleeve of her uniform. Today, she wore a pretty green dress with a floral print and brass buttons, but she hadn't forgotten to tuck a clean, white handkerchief inside the sleeve.

"Next Christmas we'll be together again. I promise," Allison added. She and Jack were sitting on the edge of the hospital bed, and he placed a comforting arm around her shoulders.

"You get well soon, Miss," sniffed Martha, "and come home to Wellington, where we can take proper care of you."

"My doctor says I should be out in a couple of days. I'll spend the weekend at Wellington, but then I must get back to work before Theo plunges the company into bankruptcy."

"I heard that," Theo said as he reentered the room and began cleaning up.

"It was a wonderful party, Theo. Thank you for everything. You and James outdid yourselves. But how did you pull it together so quickly?"

"We had a good helper-elf," Theo answered, winking at Jack.

"You were in on it, too?" Allison asked. "But you need to get ready for your mother's visit."

"You wouldn't believe what Zavie and Roberta did to my apartment before they left for Jamaica. It is completely ready, decorations, groceries, and all."

"Both of us are so blessed," Allison said. "I'm ashamed of myself for the self-pity I was feeling yesterday. No more of that nonsense."

"And no more partying for today," Jack added, standing. "Let's get you tucked into bed."

"It's four in the afternoon," she argued. "And I'm too excited to be sleepy."

"In case you've forgotten, you're in the hospital. Patients in hospitals are supposed to rest."

"I'll be going now, Miss Allison," said Martha who had been helping Theo and the caterer clean up. "Felix will have the car waiting."

"Of course, Martha. Thank you so much for coming. It has been a wonderful day."

"I'm glad I could come, Miss. It was mighty lonely at home. I'll see you in a couple of days. Oh, and thank you for the beautiful brooch," she added, touching the exquisite gold pin fastened to her collar. Earlier, Theo explained the significance of the three gems: the two small diamonds represented Allison and Martha's son, Martin, who were both born in April, and the Topaz stone was for Marc, whose birthday was in November.

"You're very welcome," Allison said, sharing a conspiratorial look with Theo. "I hope you enjoy it."

"I'll cherish it always. Goodbye now." Allison sensed that Martha was hastening to make a quick exit before the waterworks started again.

"Theo, you couldn't have found any more appropriate or meaningful gifts," Allison said after the room cleared. "Thank you so much for doing my Christmas shopping for me."

"James helped, and as you know, he has exquisite taste."

"He certainly does and so do you. What did I give *you*, by the way?"

"A red Maserati. I hope that's okay," Theo teased.

"Absolutely, as long as it's no bigger than this," Allison said, measuring the size of a Matchbox car with her fingers.

"In that case," Jack added. "I'll take a yellow Porsche."

"So, you only like me for my money. I might have guessed, Mr. Sanderling."

"Honey, you could be a worthless bum and I'd still fall head-over-heels for you. Now, it's off to bed with you." Jack gently guided her toward the bed.

"I am pretty tired, but I haven't coughed in hours. Have you noticed?"

"That's right, you haven't. No more sympathy for you, young lady. Now in you go." He lifted the covers and tucked her underneath.

"Jack, I'm so glad you were here today. I'm so glad you're in my life. I thought I had lost you forever."

"We'll never be separated again if I have anything to say about it," Jack declared as he leaned over to kiss Allison. "I'll be back tomorrow."

"I'd like to meet your mother."

"She'll be arriving the day after tomorrow. I'll bring her to see you."

"No, not here. I'll be home—at Wellington, that is—in a couple of days. I'd like you and her to come to my childhood home. It would make the holidays complete. How about the twenty-eighth? I should be home by then."

"Sure, that sounds fine," Jack said. "She'll be thrilled to meet you."

"Do you think so, really? She won't resent me for stealing her baby from her?"

"Fortunately, my younger brother paved the way, so I don't think you need to worry about her. I'll see you tomorrow. Sleep well."

"I will. Good night, Jack."

Jack leaned over to kiss her again, and Allison wished she could invite him to climb under the covers with her. They belonged together. She knew it. She felt it in the depths of her being. Could this really be happening to her? Could Allison Harmon finally have found love?

CHAPTER 36

The next morning, Allison woke up early, still wearing her beautiful silk peignoir. She hadn't run a fever for twenty-four hours, and, for the first time since arriving at the hospital, she didn't require sedation to keep her from coughing all night. Surely the doctor would release her today. She pulled the draperies open to see what was happening outside her window. Sunrise was still an hour away, and fluffy snowflakes—shimmering in the city lights—drifted from the dark heavens, piling higher and higher on the roof of the parking garage below. Today, she decided to do some important research, but first a shower was in order.

When the nurse entered to take Allison's vital signs, she found her freshly washed patient engrossed in her laptop. Allison was searching for a private detective in Manhattan. She settled on Strong Brothers, Private Investigators, for no reason other than that their office was located conveniently only a block from her building. She scanned the online reviews which, with the exception of one, labeling David Strong as "eccentric," were positive.

"Well, Ms. Jones, it looks like you may be going home tomorrow," announced the nurse.

"Really? That's wonderful!"

"The pulmonologist will be in to see you soon," the nurse said. "Then we need to take one more chest x-ray. You'll be on Prednisone and antibiotics for five more days."

"Okay, thanks."

Allison was anxious to start making phone calls immediately, but she knew it was too early in the day. She was even more anxious to get out of this place. She'd had excellent care, and the staff had been wonderful, but now that she was feeling better, the walls were closing in on her, and she desperately needed to get back to the office.

By the time Jack arrived at ten a.m., Allison had managed to check off several items from her to-do list. She dealt with numerous e-mail messages, set up an appointment with David Strong, and talked to Martha about arrangements for Saturday's dinner. She was dozing in front of CNN when Jack woke her with a tender kiss.

"Good morning, Sunshine," he crooned into her ear.

"I was just dreaming about you," she said sleepily, enfolding his neck and pulling him close for another kiss.

"You were? Was I behaving myself?"

"Not at all. It was delightful! Hey, does your Mom like salmon?" Allison asked, changing the subject without taking a breath.

"Salmon? I guess so, why?"

"I'm planning our dinner party and I want to serve foods that your mother likes."

"Dinner party? I didn't know we were coming for dinner. You're not even out of the hospital yet, and you'll still need a lot of rest after you go home."

"I'm not cooking it, just planning it," she said.

"Oh, of course. I mean… listen Allie, we come from very different worlds. My mom is from a small town. She's very… well, she's not fancy."

"I want her to feel comfortable. I want *you* to feel comfortable. I can't change the way I grew up, though, any more than you can."

"I wouldn't want you to change, but I'm still having trouble reconciling the Allie I met in Paris with Allison Harmon, the billionaire tycoon. I don't know if I can fit into your world."

"Jack, I'm not sure *I* fit into my world, but I can assure you that both women are me. The Allie that you met in Paris, the one who instantly fell in love with you, is the one I wish I could be all the time, but it's not possible. I was born into the Harmon Empire and I have responsibilities because of it. I also have great wealth and privilege because of it. But that doesn't change who I am at the core, and it doesn't mean my life is always easy. There are trade-offs."

"I'm sure there must be. I just don't want to disappoint or embarrass you."

"You couldn't possibly. Now, let's plan a wonderful meal that your mother will enjoy. Does she have a favorite wine? My father's wine cellar is well-stocked with vintage… oh, sorry."

"You, see, that's what I'm talking about. My mother buys her wine at the Winn Dixie."

"It'll be fine, Jack. I promise."

CHAPTER 37

Silvia's train pulled into Penn Station right on schedule. As the wheels screeched to a halt, Silvia's anxiety ratcheted up a notch. She and Edward had been in nearly constant communication by phone and text since they parted company in D.C. What will her eldest son think of his old Mom acting like a love struck school-girl? She hadn't thought of herself in terms of sexuality for many years. It was quite a surprise to discover that she still had urges in that department. Silvia could hardly wait to see Edward, but before they meet again, there are some important decisions to be made. What if he expected a physical relationship right away? How would she handle it? The last man she made love with was her husband, and that was nearly twenty years ago. Would she even remember how?

"Jack, Sweetheart!" Silvia spotted her handsome son.

"Hi, Mom! Welcome to New York."

"I wondered if I'd ever get here. You look thin, Darling. Are you okay?" They embraced and Jack took her luggage.

"I've lost a little weight, but I'm fine," he said. "I've been running a lot."

"You need some of your Mom's home cooking."

"You can say that again. So what's new? How are Simon and Carolyn? Any kids yet?"

The surface chatter continued until they settled in a taxi cab. After a brief moment of silence, Jack spoke again.

"Guess what, Mom. I've met someone."

"You have? That's wonderful, dear. Tell me about her."

"Well, you may have heard of her. I met her in Paris, but she lives right here in Manhattan."

"Is she famous? Is she a movie star? Oh, no, not a movie star."

"No, her name is Allison Harmon, and she's one of the richest women in the world."

"Allison Harmon. No, I've never heard of her. Are we talking old money or new?"

"Old, centuries old, it seems. Have you heard of Marcus Harmon, the textile magnate?"

"No, but he sounds very important. So, is this serious?"

"I think so. In fact, she invited us for dinner tomorrow evening. I want you to meet her and she wants to meet you."

Silvia grasped her opportunity. "Well, there's someone I want you to meet, too. His name is Edward, Edward Hastings, and he lives in Manhattan."

"Mom, you sly dog. When did this happen?"

"Three days ago on the train. He's a professor at NYU."

"Let's get you settled at the apartment, and then I want to hear all about Edward."

"You don't mind?"

"Mind? Of course not. Just take it slow until you get to know him, okay?"

"That's exactly what your brother said."

"Why don't we invite Edward to join us for dinner tomorrow night?"

"That sounds perfect. Do you think Allison will mind?"

"I think she'll love the idea, but I'll check with her first to be sure."

CHAPTER 38

More than ready to leave the hospital, Allison was thrilled to see Felix waiting for her outside the front entrance. Regardless of the fact that she felt perfectly able to walk, the nurse insisted she ride in a wheelchair from the fifth floor. All of the wilted flowers had been disposed of and the vases collected by Theo. Hundreds more arrangements were delivered to both Harmon & Harmon and Wellington Manor, according to Theo. When Allison thought about it, she realized, somewhat regretfully, that—although she is acquainted with a great many people and thousands more know who she is—she has very few real friends. It's a frequent consequence of position and fame. In fact, Allison Harmon lived a rather lonely existence. She sensed that her life was about to undergo a drastic change, but was change really possible or must she remain victim to her bloodline forever?

As the car approached the front gate of Wellington, Felix alerted Martha by cell phone, resulting in a welcoming committee of three. Martha, Gretchen, and Clarence waited on the front steps to greet her.

"Welcome home, Miss Allison," Martha said as Clarence took her luggage. "How are you feeling?"

"Much better, thanks. Gretchen, Clarence, I hope you had a nice Christmas… Oh, my!"

Stepping over the threshold, she spotted it standing proudly at the curve of the grand staircase. "A Christmas tree. It's beautiful, Clarence. Did you decorate it?"

"I had some help, Miss. Gretchen's kids stopped in and gave me a hand."

"Well, they did a wonderful job. Thank them for me, Gretchen."

Allison noticed that, unlike the last time she entered this cavernous space, there was a sensation of warmth and contentment. A decorated Christmas tree standing in the foyer certainly contributed to the welcoming atmosphere, as did the crackling fire in the drawing room, but it was more than that. She actually felt at home. While she enjoyed her spacious, exquisitely appointed condominium in the city, it never wrapped its arms around her and welcomed her home. Yes, the view from her city place—especially at night—was incredible, the services were impeccable, and its location convenient to her office building; but it didn't feel like home. It never had.

She hoped Jack and his mother would feel welcome and comfortable upon their arrival tomorrow evening. She should have invited them to spend the night. *Oh, no! Why didn't I think of it earlier?* Pneumonia must have sucked her brain cells out. *Maybe it's not too late.*

"Martha, how many bedrooms are ready for guests?"

"All of them, Miss. Why do you ask?"

"I was thinking I should have invited our dinner guests to stay the night. Would it be too much trouble for you and Gretchen?"

"Of course not. Maybe the temporary maid service could send someone to help. Shall I call?"

"Let me get in touch with Jack first. I'll let you know within the hour."

"Yes, Miss. Then you should get some rest."

"I'll take a nap this afternoon. How are the dinner preparations coming along?"

"Everything is on schedule, Miss. You needn't worry about a thing." Allison noticed that Martha had pinned her brooch to the collar of her uniform. *I'm so glad she likes it*, she thought. *Theo has great taste. I hope he's prepared to be my official Christmas gift shopper from now on.*

"Wonderful," Allison said aloud, climbing the stairs slowly. "And now, I can't believe I'm saying this, but I'm ready for that nap. But first I'll call Jack."

Reluctant, at first, Jack and Silvia finally agreed to spend the night at Wellington. Silvia couldn't speak for Edward, but she would invite him.

"I apologize for this late notice, Jack, but my hospital stay seems to have made my thinking mushy. I'm so glad you'll be staying. It'll give me a chance to get to know your mother, and it'll give her some time with Edward. How exciting that she met someone."

"Yeah, she seems to be smitten all right. They met last night for dinner and 'The Phantom.' Mom was almost floating when she came in after midnight."

"But I thought *you* were planning to take her to the show."

"I didn't mind giving my ticket to Edward—who, by the way, is quite the English gentleman. I needed to study for my orals, anyway."

"Well, I think it's sweet. I can't wait to meet them both. Felix will pick you up at five tomorrow evening, okay? Oh, I don't have your address."

Once the arrangements were settled and Martha was updated, Allison flopped on her bed, relieved to be uninterrupted by scurrying nurses who insisted on taking her blood pressure and listening to her lungs every few minutes. She fell into a deep sleep.

The next morning, Allison grabbed a cup of coffee and headed for the study. An immediate need to gather as much documentation as possible for the upcoming meeting with David Strong was pressing on her. Surely she could find something, anything, to point his search in the right direction. Perhaps Opa left some evidence behind. *There must be a record of payments to a care facility or perhaps adoption papers.*

Allison rolled her father's big leather chair across the room to the long, walnut credenza and began digging through the files stored there. Nearly two hours passed like the blink of an eye with no leads whatsoever.

"I brought you a sandwich and some coffee, Miss," Martha said, setting a tray on the round pedestal table. "I thought you might need a break."

"Okay, thanks," Allison said, absentmindedly. "Say, Martha, what was the name of the care facility in Utica where Marc was originally sent?"

"I think it was 'something Cottage'."

"Yes, Caring Cottage. That's it. I wonder if it's still there. I think I found the address."

"But if your grandfather moved Marc, how would that help?"

"They might have a record of where he was taken."

"You'll find him, Miss. I know you will. In the meantime, you need to keep up your strength. Here's some lunch for you, and it's time to take your medicine," she added, pouring a fresh cup of coffee.

"Thanks. I think I'll take it in the conservatory. After a week in the hospital, I feel sun-starved, and the sun is actually shining at the moment. I can go through another file while I eat."

Martha picked up the tray and followed Allison down the hallway, past the library and up two steps to the sunny conservatory that overlooked the pool and rear gardens. From May through August one could expect to see sunbeams glistening off the water, but this time of year the pool cover was blanketed with snow. After last night's snowfall, the entire backyard, unblemished by footprints, displayed an enchanting winter scene.

She recalled childhood holidays when she and her cousins and a few neighbor children would bundle up for an entire day of outdoor frolic. First they would use the plentiful supply of snow to build a whole family of snow people standing on the terrace. Then they would trudge through the back gardens with sleds until they reached the knoll just this side of the sound. For young children with short legs, dressed in bulky snow suits, it might as well have been Mount Everest. They would climb up one side and ride down the other again and again until their legs ached and their cheeks turned as red as sun-ripened tomatoes. *Oh, how Marc would have enjoyed the fun!* she thought. *I hope he has had a good life.*

Basking in the warm sunlight with Christmas carols piped throughout the house made Allison drowsy, and she drifted off for a few minutes. Her dream was filled with fanciful ice-sculpture people who danced about the yard in colorful tutus and skated on the frozen pool. She invited them to come in by the fire for hot chocolate, but they refused the invitation. "We drink only ice-cold lemonade," they claimed. "Hot chocolate is bad for our health. Come outside and play with us," they called to her.

"I can't. The cold air makes me cough."

Allison awakened, realizing she had been coughing in her sleep. The grandfather clock in the hallway told her she dozed for twenty minutes or so, and during that time someone had covered her legs with an afghan. She bolted upright, causing several file folders to slip to the floor, spilling their contents. "Oh bother," she exclaimed to herself. Her guests were due to arrive in a few hours, and she still needed to shower and change; but one folder caught her eye. The label read: "Endowment Fund B, 1987-Present." *1987... That's the year Marc was born.*

She swallowed a couple bites of her sandwich, picked up the folder, and leafed through it. It appeared to contain a collection of annual reports showing activity on one of her grandfather's many endowment funds. She was well aware of these investments, the interest of which had been used for donations to various charitable organizations. This practice was common among the very wealthy. In her grandfather's case, she surmised, it was likely motivated more as a tax shelter than from any true philanthropic incentive. She scanned the documents, noticing the list of annual recipients: New York City Rescue Mission; Habitat for Humanity, International; Humane Society of New York State; Morrison Group Home for the Mentally

Disabled; American Cancer Society; etc. *Wait, Morrison Group Home for the Mentally Disabled?*

Allison quickly gathered the files in her arms, slipped on her shoes, and returned to the study. A phone call was in order. Did she dare hope that Marc lived in New York City? Was it possible he lived only a few miles away all these years? With shaking hands she searched the Internet. *Here it is!* Holding her breath, she punched the numbers and waited—one ring, two rings... "Morrison Home. This is Amanda. How may I help you?"

"Uh, hello, Amanda. This is Allison Harmon. Do you have a young man named Marcus Harmon living there?"

"That name doesn't sound familiar, Ma'am, but let me check. I'm new here, and I haven't learned all the names yet."

"Okay, thanks," Allison said, trying to control her nervous anticipation.

"Ma'am?" Amanda was back on the line after a minute or two that seem more like an hour.

"Yes?"

"There's no one by that name living here. Is there anything else I can do to help?"

"No, thank you," Allison answered dejectedly and disconnected.

Disappointed, Allison placed the file on her father's desk and left his study. *It's time to get in touch with Mr. Strong and see if he can earn his fee,* she decided. *I'm getting nowhere.*

CHAPTER 39

Allison was still dressing when the long, black limousine pulled up to Wellington a bit later than expected, and Felix opened the gate by remote control. After eight hours of nearly nonstop snowfall, the Manor was a sight to behold, even in the dark. Every tree lining the long driveway was laden with layer-upon-layer of cottony fluff, causing the limbs to droop like willows weeping along a riverbank. Their powdery burden sparkled in the light of evenly spaced, flickering gas lamps.

Earlier, when Felix—who preferred to save the limo for special occasions and honored guests—ushered Silvia and Jack into the elongated sedan, mother and son gawked in amazement and a colony of butterflies took up residence in Silvia's stomach.

Silvia, who had never seen a real Rolls Royce, hoped her new dress and shoes were appropriate for the occasion and wondered whether she should have advised Edward—the next passenger to be loaded—to wear a tuxedo.

Even after Christmas, the traffic was unbelievably heavy, and the trip took nearly an hour. Edward explained to Silvia that tourism in Manhattan peaks between Christmas and New Year's Day. "One can scarcely maneuver through the crowds, especially around Rockefeller

Center," he said. Jack concurred, and, from that point forward, their conversation flowed effortlessly. Silvia was relieved to find Jack and Edward at ease in each other's company.

Now, approaching the imposing palatial structure before her, Silvia's anxiety returned. Into what foreign realm has her son inserted himself? Will she embarrass him? Will he embarrass himself? She wanted to run in the opposite direction, but it was too late to retreat. Why did she agree to spend the night? Passing a few hours as a dinner guest was one thing, but staying overnight required extended social refinement and increased one's chances of making a blunder. She must try not to sound like a hillbilly. Silvia had found that some northerners automatically associated a southern accent with ignorance. Of course, southerners held their own preconceived notions regarding New Yorkers and *their* dialects, but still, she would try to take special care with her grammar *and* her manners this evening.

The limousine came to a stop in front of the ostentatious stone edifice, where a tall man dressed in a regal uniform was waiting on the front portico. He took the guests' overnight bags and ushered them inside. Upon crossing the threshold, Silvia felt like she had been transported onto a 1930's movie set, but this movie was in living color. Not since taking her class on a field trip to Hotel Roanoke had she entered a more magnificent foyer. Her entire house could probably fit into this massive vestibule with its inlaid marble floor, grand mahogany staircase, and expensive artwork, all lit by an enormous crystal chandelier and ornate wall sconces. A sixteen-foot Christmas tree decorated with twinkling lights and Spode china ornaments completed the breathtaking tableau.

Once inside, an older woman warmly greeted the guests and introduced herself as Martha, the housekeeper. She took their coats and invited them into the drawing room to thaw out in front of a mesmerizing fire. Immediately, another servant offered them a choice of spiced cider or hot toddy. Martha said her name was Gretchen and instructed them to request anything of her that they might need. "Dinner will be served at seven," she announced as Gretchen served the steaming beverages and fresh canapés.

Within minutes of their arrival, Allison descended the staircase, looking stunning but surprisingly casual. Granted, her perfectly-fitted jeans were Versace and her red sweater was made of Chinese cashmere, but she appeared relaxed and rested. Her straightened hair looked freshly washed and shiny, but not like she spent a lot of time styling it. Her simple jewelry consisted of gold hoop earrings. As soon as the young woman spotted Jack sitting next to the fireplace, Silvia saw the corners of her mouth lift. *There's definitely a spark between these two*, she thought. *Who could blame my son for being attracted to her? She's gorgeous.*

"Welcome, everyone!" Allison said cheerfully, crossing the foyer to the large but warmly inviting drawing room. Jack stood and placed his mug on the coffee table. "You look beautiful," Jack said to her quietly. Silvia knew those words were meant only for Allison, but she couldn't help overhearing her son and noticing his loving tone of voice. After depositing a light kiss on her cheek he handled the introductions.

"Allie, this is my Mom, Silvia Sanderling, and her friend, Dr. Edward Hastings."

"I'm so happy to meet you, Mrs. Sanderling," Allison said, taking Silvia's hand, "and you, Dr. Hastings."

"Call me Silvia, please."

"And I'm just Edward. How kind of you to include me."

Allie took a seat on the divan and motioned for the men to be seated. "I'm glad you could come. How was your ride from the city?"

"Luxurious," Silvia gushed, unabashed. "I've never ridden in a limousine before."

"Oh, that." Allison said, seeming embarrassed. "I thought of selling the Rolls, but Felix takes such wonderful care of my father's vehicles. He enjoys showing off his handiwork."

"Your home is exquisite," Silvia said.

"Thanks, but I can't really take credit for it. It has been in the family since before I was born, and my mother did all of the renovating and decorating. Technically speaking, I don't even live here. I have a condo in the city. It's much closer to my office."

"Yes, Jack mentioned that, but I wonder how you can stay away from such an enchanting house," Silvia said, gesturing in a broad circle.

"Indeed," Edward said. "It reminds me of a country manor I once visited in Cornwall."

"Actually, it's fashioned after the Wellington Estate in Ireland. There's quite a rich history associated with it," Allison said.

"Ah yes, Lord Wellington," exclaimed Edward.

"You know of the Duke?" Allison asked.

"Only a bit from my childhood history lessons," Edward said. "I believe he fought against Napoleon at Waterloo, if memory serves.

Would it be forward of me to ask for a tour? Old houses have always intrigued me."

"Not at all. I'd be happy to walk you through after dinner, and please help yourself to the library if you'd care to learn more about the Duke. There are several interesting volumes in the history section."

"Wonderful," Silvia said. "I'd love to see the rest of the house, too." Then, changing the subject, she added, "Jack tells us you've been quite ill, Allison. How are you feeling?"

"Much better, thanks. It's not fun being hospitalized on Christmas Day, but the experience opened my eyes to the plight of patients and medical personnel, alike, during the holidays. I'm so thankful for the wonderful care I received."

The increasingly comfortable conversation continued until Martha entered to announce that dinner was ready.

"Thank you, Martha," Allison said, then, rising, she addressed the group. "Shall we move to the dining room? I hope you brought hearty appetites. Martha's cooking is amazing."

As Martha crossed the foyer, the couples followed her. She opened the French doors to the massive dining room to reveal a breathtaking scene. Silvia tried to restrain her and "oohs!" and "ahs!" but the long table was spectacular with its fine linen table cloth, napkins folded to look like roses, silver candelabras, and multiple arrangements of actual red roses adorned with sprigs of holly. Gleaming silver chargers awaited the first course, and delicate Waterford crystal stemware sparkled in the candlelight. The fireplace mantle and sideboard were tastefully decorated to coordinate with the table, and the fire cast a cheerful glow throughout the expansive hall. On a table intended to seat up to twenty diners, a mere four place settings might easily be obscured, except that Martha's decorating expertise created a continuous tableau from one end to the other.

"Martha, everything looks beautiful! Thank you for all of your preparations," Allison said as Jack and Edward assisted the women with their chairs.

"Yes," added Silvia. "Thank you for making us so welcome."

"It's my pleasure, Ma'am, but I had a lot of help."

"Call me Silvia, please. Ma'am makes me feel like I'm back home with my fourth graders."

"Yes, Ma'am... I mean, Silvia." As Martha began to fill the wine glasses, a door leading to the kitchen swung open and Gretchen entered carrying a tray of crisp salads.

"What's that amazing aroma coming from the kitchen?" Silvia said.

"I'm preparing poached salmon, but it's probably the truffle risotto that you smell. I hope you enjoy everything."

"Truffles. Well, I, for one, could get used to this kind of treatment," Silvia declared in her most pronounced southern accent. "Son, I do believe you've found yourself a keeper."

"Allie certainly knows how to treat her guests, doesn't she?" Jack agreed, patting Allison's hand affectionately.

"I was talking about Martha," Silvia joked, instantly regretting her attempt at humor so early in the evening. She hoped Allison hadn't taken offense. Fortunately, everyone, including Allison, laughed at her witticism, and Allison raised her wine glass.

"A toast to Martha," she declared.

Martha, looking pleased, but embarrassed by the attention, retreated toward the kitchen. "Maybe you should save the toasting until *after* you've tasted my cooking," she quipped.

Jack stood and raised his glass. "I'd like to propose a toast to our generous—and beautiful—hostess," he said, looking admiringly at Allison.

"Here, here!" agreed Edward, rising to join Jack.

"Thank you. I'm so happy you all could come. And now, before we sample Martha's handiwork, I'd like to say a blessing. Please be seated."

As Allison offered a prayer of gratitude for her restored health, as well as for good food and friends with whom to share it, Silvia considered the prospect of this young woman as a future daughter-in-law. She wondered if her son had thought through the ramifications of such a dichotomous union. Perhaps Jack found himself wondering if his mother might be considering marriage to the charming Professor Hastings and, if so, how they might resolve the long-distance issue.

After a sumptuous four-course dinner, accompanied by lively conversation, Allison fulfilled her promise of a guided tour, starting with the wine cellar, the entrance to which was completely invisible. Beside the grand staircase, behind the Christmas tree, a door was artfully concealed within the intricate wood trim that spanned from the floor to a height above Allison's head. Entrance to the hidden staircase was accessed by pressing a specific panel in just the right spot. To everyone's amazement, a pocket door slid out of sight revealing the stairs to the cellar.

"Oh, my," Edward said. "This old house seems to hold one fascinating feature after another."

As Allison led her guests down the steep staircase, she explained that the original structure built on this property once served as a stop along the Underground Railroad. "Many runaway slaves from the southern plantations of North and South Carolina were hidden in what is now our wine cellar. History books mention only North Castle in this vicinity, but my grandfather came upon some papers that identified Wellington as a stopover organized by the manor's black servants at the time. A well-kept secret from the owners, it was never officially acknowledged by historians."

"Fascinating," Edward said. "I know so little about the American Civil War era, having been raised in the U.K. I should like to learn more."

"As a Virginia native, I'm afraid I know more than I care to when it comes to slavery," Silvia said. "Of course, it's important to 'remember history lest we repeat it,' as someone once said, but I find the whole concept of slavery so abhorrent that it makes me feel ashamed of my southern roots."

"Excuse me for one moment while I select a bottle of champagne for later," Allison interjected. Then, noticing the shared reaction of her guests to the substantial collection before them, she explained, "My father and grandfather were quite the oenophiles, as you can see. They amassed more wine than they could have consumed in two lifetimes. Actually, I think they enjoyed collecting it more than drinking it. Anyway, I hope each of you will take a couple of bottles when you leave. Just tell Gretchen what you prefer. The reds are there, at the far end, and the whites are stored against the outside wall where the temperature stays cooler."

"I see quite an extensive selection of Ports on these shelves," observed Edward. "Why, some are as old as twenty years."

"Yes, when Daddy discovered that Port was being made in countries other than Portugal, he began collecting them from all around the globe. Some have been aged in wooden kegs and then bottled. Others are bottle-aged. He has at least two of every rare vintage since 1980 or so… one for drinking and another for collecting. He enjoyed comparing them, and, in the end, decided nothing could surpass the quality of those from the Douro Valley where Port has been made for 2,000 years."

"You seem well versed in the art of vinification, Allison," Edward said.

"Only what I learned from my father. I haven't really made a study of it, myself."

"You must miss him a great deal," Silvia said, noticing Allison's downcast expression whenever her father was mentioned.

"I do. The house seems so empty without him, especially at Christmas."

"Where does that lead?" Jack asked, pointing to a second staircase at the far end of the cellar.

"Oh, that goes to the original servants' quarters and the kitchen. We've assumed that's how the slaves were smuggled in."

"Fascinating," Edward said. "May we see?"

"Of course, but be careful, the stairs are treacherous."

Switching on another light, Allison led the group up the steep passageway and through a door which opened into a very pleasant sitting room.

"Wow," Silvia said. "These are servants' quarters?"

"Martha lives here now. You see, when Martha lost her family in an accident..."

"Oh, how dreadful," Silvia said.

"Yes, it was a terrible loss. Anyway, Daddy had this whole area converted into a suite for Martha, who practically raised me."

"I see," Silvia said. "I sensed that Martha was more than just a housekeeper."

"She's been more like a mother to me, actually."

"She certainly can't complain about her living quarters," Edward said, looking around. "This looks very comfortable, indeed."

"I hope it is. She has a good-sized bedroom and a bathroom through there." Allison motioned toward an alcove at the rear of the space. "And this leads to the kitchen, which of course, she can use for her own meals as well as ours... mine, that is. I try to come for dinner every Saturday evening."

The kitchen was huge, surprisingly modern and equipped with commercial grade appliances. Martha, Gretchen, and two maids were still cleaning up from dinner.

"Oh, hello, everyone," Martha said, looking surprised to see house guests in the kitchen.

"I was just giving our guests a tour of the house," Allison said. "I hope you don't mind, Martha. We passed through your apartment on the way from the wine cellar."

"Of course not, Miss," Martha said.

Then, handing the champagne to Gretchen, Allison asked her to put the bottle on ice.

"Dinner was outstanding, Martha. Thank you," Allison said.

"I'll second that," chimed Jack, enthusiastically, as Edward and Silvia added their compliments.

"Well, you've seen the dining room. Shall we move on to the conservatory?" Allison asked, leading the way through the foyer, down a wide corridor, past the study and up two steps.

"Okay, this is definitely my favorite room," Silvia said, swirling around to take in the entire airy space. "The view, by daylight, must be gorgeous."

"I wish you could see it in the summer. The rear gardens are quite spectacular, thanks to Clarence."

"Maybe we could be talked into a return visit," Silvia said, privately elbowing Jack.

Allison switched on the outside floodlight. "Of course you'd be welcome, and judging by the snow, you made the right decision to spend the night."

"Surely Clarence doesn't take care of the entire property alone," Edward said.

"Oh, no. He has more than one lawn service to help him. But he supervises the work and maintains the greenhouse himself. It's his pride and joy."

"Does Clarence live on the property?" Jack asked.

"Yes, he and his wife occupy the caretaker's cottage just over there," Allison said, pointing toward a grove of snow-covered trees to the east. "Shall we have our champagne in here later?"

"Yes, please," Silvia said. "I claim that comfortable looking chair by the fireplace. Is the entire house heated by these wood fireplaces, Allison?"

"Not any more. Clarence builds the wood fires to make it cozy for guests, but we have a modern heat pump, and the upstairs fireplaces have been converted to natural gas. So, please feel free to adjust your thermostats according to your comfort. Here, let me show you the study and the library. Excuse the mess. I've been doing some research."

"Does the research have anything to do with your brother?" Jack asked.

"You have a brother?" Silvia said before Allison had a chance to respond to the first question. "I thought you were an only child."

"I thought so, too, until a few weeks ago. It seems my parents kept his existence a secret for over twenty-five years."

"Where's he been all these years?" Edward asked.

"That's the question I hope a private detective will be able to answer."

"So you hired someone?" Jack asked.

"Yes, I'm meeting him tomorrow, as a matter of fact. I thought I could ride into the city when Felix takes you all home. My appointment isn't until two, so we can sleep as late as we want in the morning."

"I hope you find him, Allison," Silvia said with genuine solicitude. "As an only child, myself, I understand how important family connections are. Is he younger or older than you?"

"He would be nearly two years younger. I haven't seen him since I was about twenty months old, so I don't really remember him."

"How did you discover his existence?" Edward asked. Then, as if remembering his manners, he added, "Perhaps we're being too intrusive."

Silvia agreed. "Yes, dear. I apologize."

"Not at all," Allison reassured them. "Jack knows the whole story, and I'm happy to share the details with you. Let me show you Daddy's library. Then, we'll settle in the conservatory for that glass of champagne, and I'll start from the beginning."

CHAPTER 40

By the time Allison finished the account of her long-lost brother, it was nearly midnight. "Now I've kept my guests up too late," she said contritely.

"No," Silvia and Edward chimed in unison. Then Silvia added, "It has been a most interesting bedtime story—definitely worth staying awake for!"

"You're the one who should be getting to bed, Allie. You did just get out of the hospital, as I recall," Jack stated in a tone more protective than domineering.

"I'm fine, but we didn't get to finish our tour. Let me take you to your rooms and we can resume the show-and-tell tomorrow."

"That sounds great," Silvia said. "It's hard to believe there could be more to this grand palace than what we've already seen."

"It is grand, I suppose, but still, it's just a house," Allison said. "Especially when I'm alone here, it can be a big, empty, lonely house. Family and friends are what make a house a home, and I thank you for helping me feel at home this evening. I haven't experienced that sensation since my father's death."

Jack's smile reflected a mixture of compassion and pride, also satisfaction that the evening had gone so well. Swelling in his chest was a sense of admiration for his mother, who, without apology, personified her humble roots. At the same time, he felt proud of Allison, who had proven to be charming, down-to-earth, and generous. For the first time since discovering Allison's true identity, Jack thought it might actually be possible for their distinctly divergent worlds to merge gracefully.

As they climbed the long, curving staircase to the second floor, Allison mentioned that coffee, juice, and cinnamon rolls would be available in the dining room whenever they chose to rise in the morning. "If you enjoyed Martha's cooking this evening, wait till you taste her homemade cinnamon rolls. They are divine."

"If this treatment keeps up, I'm going to need a diet and a gym membership in the New Year," Silvia said.

"The rear view looks quite satisfactory to me," Edward—who was walking behind Silvia—declared salaciously.

"Hey, you two!" Jack laughed. "Some of us are too young and innocent to hear that kind of talk."

"We may be old, but we're not dead," declared Silvia, playfully patting her son on the rump.

Upon reaching the landing, Allison delivered the room assignments. The group exchanged good-nights and hugs. Then, as four bedroom doors closed for the night, each occupant entertained the same thought: how much more comfortably they would sleep in two fewer luxurious en suites.

CHAPTER 41

The morning of December thirtieth brought both bright sunshine and deep snow surrounding Wellington's sturdy walls. The male guests occupying the front suites were awakened at seven a.m. by Clarence and two other workers blowing snow into high drifts along the circular driveway. In the center, another pile completely obscured the fountain. Jack decided to stay in bed a while longer with his laptop. With his orals only days away, he needed to take advantage of every opportunity to study. By the time Allison and Silvia descended the stairs at nine a.m., Jack had moved to the dining room where both he and Edward were working on their second cups of coffee and who-knows-how-many of Martha's scrumptious cinnamon rolls. "Since I was the first to rise this morning," Edward was saying to Jack, "I have already spent nearly an hour in the library. What an inviting room it is. I felt like a small child in a candy store unable to choose from the wide selection. I am especially impressed with the extensive collection of first editions."

As Jack glanced up from his breakfast, he was caught off guard by the sight of Allie floating down the staircase, wearing a deep blue dressing gown of silk that clung in all the right places. Every time he saw her, he fell more in love with her and, except for their initial meeting in Paris, more attracted to her. Observing her ease with house guests, especially his mother, reassured him that any previous misgivings were unfounded. Of course, the couple wouldn't rush into a permanent union. That would be reckless, especially before he even landed a job. But Jack couldn't imagine spending the rest of his life with anyone else. From the adoring way she looked at him, he knew in his heart that Allie shared his sentiment.

"Good morning," Allison said, crossing the foyer to the dining room. "I hope everyone slept well."

"If we didn't, there are no excuses," Edward answered for the group. "I, for one, couldn't have been more comfortable in a five-star hotel."

"That's for sure," Sylvia said. "Have y'all looked outside? I've never seen so much snow in my whole life! Why, if we got this much snow in Virginia, the schools would be closed for an entire month!" Then, moving to the front window and pulling back the draperies, she added, "It really is pretty, though."

"It's only pretty if you admire it from inside, hunkered down next to the fireplace," Jack said.

"Honey, when you were a kid, you and Simon prayed all winter for snow."

"Yeah, but that was just so we could stay home from school."

"My school was never closed," Allison said, pouring two cups of coffee. "Shall we take our coffee to the conservatory, Silvia?"

"Yes, please. I'm anxious to see it in the daylight."

"Be sure to sample the cinnamon rolls," Edward said. "They're brilliant!"

"Melt-in-your-mouth brilliant," Jack concurred.

"After last night's dinner, I really shouldn't," Silvia said, reaching for the silver tongs. "But, they do look irresistible."

"I'll have Gretchen bring us some fruit."

"Yes, fruit would be good… negates the effects of… wickedness, right?"

"Of course," Allison agreed, smiling mischievously.

"Well, I prefer my wickedness to remain pure and unadulterated," Edward said.

"Yes, pure and unadulterated," Jack agreed, stuffing another roll in his mouth.

As the fires of Wellington Manor gradually died down to embers, its inhabitants spent a most pleasant morning, relaxing and enjoying each other's company. Allison completed the guided tour that began the previous evening, showing her guests three more en suites, including the spacious master suite that Jack knew she hadn't yet had the heart to occupy, plus the upstairs sitting room, and finally, a fully equipped exercise room.

"I suppose we should get dressed and prepare to head back into the city," Allison said, closing the door to the home gym.

"If we must." Edward sighed. "I confess, I could get used to this place."

"I hope you'll come back soon," Allison said. "This old house hasn't felt so alive in months—years, really."

"It would be a pleasure," Edward said, taking Allison's hand and kissing it. "I've had the most delightful weekend, my dear."

"It has been lovely, Allison. Thank you for inviting us," Silvia added. "You've been a gracious hostess, and this visit has allowed all of us to get better acquainted."

"Yes, thank you, Allie," Jack said, kissing her cheek, but longing to take her in his arms.

"Actually, Silvia and I have hatched a plan to get us all together again soon," Allie said, sharing a conspiratorial look with Silvia. "Let's get dressed and pack our bags. Martha will have lunch ready shortly, and we can share our idea."

CHAPTER 42

Carrying a briefcase brimming with disorganized files, Allison entered the offices of David Strong and Associates a few minutes before the appointed time. It was uncharacteristic of her to arrive at any meeting unprepared, but after reaching a dead end with the Caring Cottage and the Morrison Home, she had no idea how to proceed.

The secretary announced Allison's arrival, and before she had a chance to settle in the waiting room, Mr. Strong's office door opened forcefully and he swooped into the waiting area like a lightning bolt, hand outstretched. "Ms. Harmon, it's a pleasure," he shouted. "Please, come in!" He grabbed the lump of outerwear that she had just removed and handed it to his secretary without even glancing in her direction. "Here, Teresa will take your things." Teresa jumped up from her desk just in time to catch Allison's coat-hat-scarf-gloves bundle before it hit the floor. As Allison was whisked into Strong's office, she felt like the wind had been knocked out of her.

"Thank y—"

"Sit here," he barked, motioning toward the only chair other than the one behind his desk. "Now, let's get started, shall we?"

"Um, okay," Allison answered hesitantly, taken aback by the man's odd behavior. She had never met anyone like him. A middle-aged whirlwind of energy, obviously he had not been taught to use his inside voice. He darted about the room like a dragonfly, making it hard for Allison to focus her eyes in the dimly lit space. Finally, she gave up and stared at her hands that were grasping the briefcase.

"Start from the beginning, Ms. Harmon! I understand you're trying to find your brother! How long has he been missing?" Strong asked, leaning against his cluttered desk.

"Oh, well… you see…" she began.

"No, I'm afraid I don't! That's why I need to hear the whole story!" He was on his feet and darting about again. Allison felt like she couldn't gather her thoughts.

"Mr. Strong," she said, louder than she intended. He stopped his frantic pacing and turned to face her.

"Oh, dear, I'm sorry, Ms. Harmon. I'm afraid my medication is wearing off. Sometimes I make it through the entire afternoon and sometimes I don't. It's a real crap shoot."

"Medication?" she asked tentatively, wondering what kind of looney bin she had entered. "Listen, maybe we should reschedule."

"No, no. I just need a booster pill. Teresa is supposed to alert me when she sees it coming, but she tells me I don't usually give her a chance." Noticing the look of alarm on Allison's face—actually, it was the first time since her arrival that he even looked at her face—he added, "Don't worry, Ms. Harmon, I'm not dangerous. It's just ADHD." He was still shouting as he opened a desk drawer and removed a bottle of pills.

Consciously trying to relax what she guessed must be a wild expression, she asked, "ADHD? What's that?"

"Attention Deficit Hyperactivity Disorder," he explained, between gulps of water to wash down a tiny pill. "I've had it my whole life, and my doctors still haven't figured out the magic formula to keep it under control. I have good days and bad days, and the worst part is that I don't even know when I'm spiraling out of control until someone tells me or worse, looks at me like you just did."

"I'm sorry. It's just that I've never met…"

"Someone who looks like he's about to skin you alive?"

"Something like that." Allison laughed, relaxing a bit.

"Listen, Ms. Harmon, I'm really good at what I do, and if anyone can find your brother, I can." He was still talking too loudly, but finally sitting. Allison noticed that he grasped the edge of his desk so tightly his knuckles turned white. "I'll be calmer in a few minutes and we can start over, okay?"

"Okay, sure… and please, call me Allison."

"And I'm David. Now, tell me what you know and show me what you've brought."

Allison opened the briefcase and started at the beginning. She showed him the file of documents and some account ledgers that she found in her father's study. She shared her mother's letter and the photographs from the safe deposit box, all of which he instructed Teresa to copy. Finally, she recounted Martha's narrative from a few days before. As the appointment proceeded, Strong grew visibly calmer and quieter. By the time their meeting drew to a close, he had taken on a totally different persona, and Allison felt a little more confidence in his skills as an investigator.

"I'll get right on this assignment, Allison, and before you know it, you and your brother will be reunited. Teresa will take your payment before you leave, and I'll call you as soon as I have anything."

"Thanks very much," Allison said, pumping David's hand excitedly. "I'm counting on you."

CHAPTER 43

"So, Sugar, what do you think about the party? Do you like the idea?" Silvia was washing a head of lettuce as Jack emerged from the bathroom where he had just showered.

"More importantly, what's for dinner? Something smells great," Jack answered, drying his hair with a hand towel and tossing it on the counter.

"Don't change the subject or I won't feed you at all," Silvia said.

"You wouldn't withhold food from your starving baby boy, would you, Mama?" Jack said, nuzzling his mother's neck playfully.

"First of all, you're not my baby. Simon is."

"Ouch, that hurts," he said with mock insult.

"And secondly, I really want to know if you're okay with the party."

"It sounds like you and Allie have it all planned without my approval." He tried to sound offended, but he was actually very pleased by the nearly instant connection between Allie and his mom.

"Allie really wants to do it for you, and it'll give her—and me—a chance to meet your friends," Silvia said. "Besides, earning your doctorate is a big deal. You *deserve* a celebration."

"I suppose so. Hey, Zavie and Roberta will be home by then. I think Zavie and Allie will like each other don't you?"

"Absolutely. What's not to like?" Silvia said.

"So, you and Allie seem to have hit it off. Does that mean you approve?" Jack carefully avoided eye contact.

"Honey, she's a ray of sunshine and so down-to-earth for a rich gal. But do you think you can fit into her world? It's a might removed from the one you grew up in," she said in a deliberately exaggerated southern drawl.

"Like you said, she's down-to-earth," he replied, setting plates and silverware on the island. "Time will tell, but I think she might be *the one.*"

"Well, Dr. Bachelor, I'd say it's about time. Now let's eat."

CHAPTER 44

Allison left David Strong's office feeling like she had just worked up a sweat in her cycling class at the gym. Thankfully, he finally settled down a bit and convinced her of his competence, but the hyper-speed of his speech and movements left her exhausted. With so much catching up to do at the office, she had originally planned to spend a few hours there this evening, but changed her mind and instructed Felix to take her home. *I'll stop for take-out and turn in early*, she decided. Allison had kept in close touch with Theo and her vice presidents by phone, text, and email both during her hospitalization and since her release. Monday morning would be soon enough to resume her usual demanding schedule.

Upon entering her building, the doorman greeted her enthusiastically. "Welcome back Ms. Harmon. I hope you're feeling better."

"Yes, thank you, George."

"Here, let me take that for you," he said, reaching for her overnight bag.

"I'm fine. It's not heavy."

"Are you sure?" he asked, noticing the Chinese take-out bag in her other hand and the computer brief case slung over her shoulder. "You seem to be loaded down."

"Really, I'm fine. If you could just push the elevator button…"

"Of course."

Riding the elevator to the penthouse, Allison started to feel an aching loneliness creeping into her chest. The last couple of days at Wellington brought to mind happier days, before her mother's illness, when her parents or grandparents would throw parties or host overnight guests at the manor. After careful instructions in proper etiquette, Allie would be allowed to mingle with the adults until her bedtime. Even after she was sent to bed, the little girl adored listening to the music, conversation, and laughter as muffled sounds drifted upstairs to her bedroom. Sometimes she would tiptoe to the landing in her nightgown, attempting to prolong the merriment until her heavy eyelids prevented further eavesdropping.

Allison set her bag down in front of her door and punched in the combination. As the door swung open, she surveyed the vast expanse of her condominium, her eyes settling on the wall of windows at the opposite end, floor-to-ceiling windows overlooking Central Park. Lights were beginning to glisten throughout the city beyond. Any young woman in her right mind would jump at the chance to live in such a luxurious space in one of the most prestigious neighborhoods of Manhattan. So, why did coming home leave her feeling cold and empty?

In an effort to lighten her mood, Allison switched on the intercom to pipe upbeat music throughout the condo. As usual, her cleaning service left the apartment sparkling with everything in its proper place. For some reason, Allie wanted to toss her belongings in every direction. She threw her coat over the back of the white tufted sectional, flung her hat on the nearest chair, and set her dinner on the glass coffee table. Her scarf slipped to the floor and her boots followed. She padded to the kitchen, opened the refrigerator, and started pouring a glass of chardonnay, then changed her mind and settled on a pinot noir from the wine rack. The carton of beef and broccoli seemed plenty hot, so she set her wine glass on the coffee table and followed the long, wide hallway to her bedroom to find a comfortable lounging outfit. Selecting a pair of red and navy plaid flannel pajama bottoms and a long-sleeved T-shirt covered with pink hearts, she stripped down to her panties and pulled on her mismatched ensemble. Fuzzy slippers in lime green completed the outfit. When Allison caught a glimpse of herself in the full-length mirror, she laughed aloud at the ridiculous sight.

"Perfect!" she pronounced to the comical image staring back at her. Grabbing an elastic band from the dresser tray, she pulled her hair into a messy ponytail, removed her contact lenses in favor of glasses, and strode back to the great room, her slippers skating along the smooth hardwood floor. Settling into the corner of the sofa, she dove into her dinner with chopsticks minus plate or napkin.

Halfway through the meal, Allison found herself longing to talk to Jack. *Good grief,* she thought. *I just saw him a few hours ago. I must really have a bad case of lovesickness.* The feeling was still so foreign to her that she hadn't learned how to handle it. *I can't call him. Silvia is making meatloaf—his favorite—tonight. I mustn't interrupt what little mother-son time they have left.* Finally, she decided to spend the remainder of the evening planning Jack's party. She needed to extend the invitations as soon as possible. With so little lead-time, email messages and phone calls would have to suffice. She started by composing the guest list. *I wonder if I can hire a DJ or a band on such short notice.* The new focus took her mind off her loneliness, and the long icicles hanging off the balcony railing provided inspiration for a theme. *I can't pull this off without Theo's help,* she decided.

"Honey, what on earth are you wearing, and what, in God's name, have you done to your hair?" Theo asked when they connected by video phone. Allison always marveled at the ease with which Theo was able to switch gears between his employee-self and his friend-self.

"Never mind my appearance. I need your help, and James's, too," Allison said.

"You can say that again," James chimed in as he caught a glimpse of her over Theo's shoulder.

"Hey, don't be mean," she said with mock-insult. "I'm expressing a chilled-out version of Allison Harmon this evening. I kind of like it." She struck a confident pose for their benefit.

"Doll, if you need a disguise any time soon, this is it," James said.

Once the three of them got down to business, the hours ticked by quickly. Allison's loneliness was temporarily dispelled, and before ten p.m. a fitting celebration had been planned. She hoped Jack would be pleased.

CHAPTER 45

By Wednesday, Allison was a bit more caught up at work and satisfied that the party preparations were on schedule for Saturday. *A garden party would have been lovely*, she thought, *but of course, impossible in January*. Martha and Gretchen, with the help of a cleaning service, polished the Manor from top to bottom and prepared the bedrooms for overnight guests. Simon and Carolyn were invited to spend the weekend, as well as Zavie and Roberta, who were due to arrive home from Jamaica on Thursday.

Clarence hired a snow-removal company to clear the driveway and remove as much excess snow as possible. Otherwise, parking more than a half dozen cars would be impossible.

Allison was able to secure the services of a disc jockey, and Theo and James managed to contact everyone on Jack's guest list: a few special professors that mentored him through the years, his faculty advisor, some fellow doctoral candidates, and a number of colleagues from various museums throughout the city. James and Theo would arrive at Wellington early Saturday morning to direct the florist and decorators, and Martha had the caterers and temporary maids under control. Allison instructed everyone to spare no expense in the preparations. She wanted Jack's party to be a celebration fit for a king.

Thankfully, Jack passed his orals with flying colors, and, along with eleven other doctoral candidates, was presented a brown-trimmed hood signifying his new title of Doctor of Fine Arts. He was accompanied to the ceremony by his most ardent supporters: Silvia, Edward, Simon, Carolyn, Zavie, Roberta, and, of course, Allie.

At one p.m. Felix was waiting to transport the group to Wellington Manor. Allie trusted that everything had gone according to her careful plans. She realized how very fortunate she was to have two such reliable assistants as Theo and Martha, especially during this particular week when she has had to make an unexpected trip to Edinburgh.

Allison and Zach Grayson boarded the company jet Wednesday morning and, with scarcely enough time to experience jetlag, were on their way back to the States by Friday. "We can't let this debacle leak to the press, Zach. It will be blown out of proportion and make H & H appear to be environmentally irresponsible. How did it get to the point of an indictment, anyway?"

"I was as blindsided as you were," Zach said. "Our Scottish operatives repeatedly assured me the situation was under control. The summons for you to appear in court was a complete surprise to both of us."

"We were lucky it turned out to be a misinterpretation of a local ordinance," said an exhausted Allison. "H & H has always been careful about properly disposing of chemicals. Still, bad press, whether true or not, holds the power to make or break a company."

"I think it would be wise to schedule a press conference as soon as possible," said Zach. "Do you agree?"

"Absolutely. But it'll have to wait until Monday."

The most frustrating part of Allison's week was her separation from Jack. She had seen him once since the previous Saturday—only long enough to have coffee and discuss David Strong's investigation.

Being away from Jack for any length of time was becoming more and more difficult. *I've fallen in love with this man. I want him in my life forever, and he made it clear he feels the same way about me.* For the first time, the idea of marriage had entered the realm of possibility. But there was so much to consider. How would they handle the complicated financial situation? Where would they live? When and where will Jack find a job, and when he does, how would the couple deal with separate careers, especially if Jack's work took him away from the city, or worse yet, out of the country? Before they even considered getting engaged, they needed to talk about all of these issues, but when? Their time together was constantly interrupted or delayed. And, of course, Allison must locate her brother. Nothing else in her life could fall into place until she found Marc.

"So, what did Mr. Strong say? Does he have any leads?" Jack asked, sipping a latte.

"Yes," Allie said excitedly. "He thinks there's a strong—if you'll pardon the pun—possibility that Marc is at the Morrison Home after all."

"But, I thought you already checked it out."

"I did, but David thinks my grandfather changed Marc's name after my mother discovered he had been taken to the Caring Cottage.

His initial investigation has shown that there are two young men at the Morrison Home whose ages could coincide with Marc's."

"That's great news, Allie! So, all you have to do is look up their birthdates, right?"

"It's not that simple. David says their records are sealed. I'll have to hire a lawyer to subpoena the administrators to open the records. Even then, the law may stand firm, depending upon how Opa managed to get Marc's record sealed. Oh, Jack, what if he's been living right here in the city all along, but I can't ever prove he's my brother?"

"Don't start worrying. It sounds like Strong has already made some good progress. Give him a chance to earn his fee."

"You're right, of course. It's just so hard to be patient now that Marc's whereabouts feel within reach."

"We'll find him, Allie. If it takes the rest of our lives, we'll find him."

"Thank you for caring and for being my rock through this ordeal," Allie said, taking his hand in hers.

"I love you, Allie," Jack said, meeting her glistening eyes with his.

"Do you, Jack? Do you really love me?"

"More than anything."

"I love you, too. I never saw this coming, but I love you, too." Jack raised her hand to his lips and kissed it with the same fervor that he was kissing her entire body in her imagination. She wished he could take her to his apartment right this minute and turn her vivid recurring dream into reality. She wondered if Jack shared her longing for intimacy.

"Do you mean you never saw a relationship in your future? I thought all little girls dreamed of falling in love and getting married, either that or becoming a princess."

"I've been focused on the business since I was five years old. I never even had a serious boyfriend in high school. Then, in college, between working with Daddy and earning my degrees, I was too busy for a relationship. I had a few dates, of course, but the idea of a romantic relationship never crossed my mind; besides, I've never been able to trust that someone might care about me for anything other than my wealth."

"Do you trust *me?*"

"Of course I do."

"I want to marry you, Allie. I want us to be together always."

"And just how do you propose to support me, Dr. Sanderling?"

"Hey, I'm being serious here."

"I know, but I need to get back to the office, and you have to meet Zavie and Roberta at the airport. This conversation will have to resume later. After your family leaves, we can sit down and talk seriously about everything, okay?"

"Okay, deal, but don't think you're getting out of it."

"I don't want to get out of it..." she said, nibbling his ear seductively. "...just postpone it." As they stood to put on their coats, Jack glanced at the people the next table over who were staring at them and whispering. "Hum, I'm not sure I'll ever get used to *that.*"

"You don't like it?" she said, thinking he was referring to her amorous gesture.

"Not you." He pulled on his titillated earlobe and nodded in the direction of the uninvited attention. "*That.*"

"I know. It can be annoying, but it's mostly harmless curiosity."

CHAPTER 46

Saturday morning brought cloudy skies, but at forty-one degrees, the temperature was warmer than it had been all week. The hooding ceremony was fine, but Allison could have done without the long speeches. She was anxious to get to Wellington and check on the party preparations. She was so proud of Jack, who looked very handsome in his gown and tam, and like Silvia, she beamed at him with unabashed pride throughout the ceremony.

Later, as Jack and his enthusiasts were piling into the limousine, Allison's cell phone vibrated. "Excuse me while I take this. It's David Strong."

Aware of how important Strong's investigation was to Allison, the passengers turned their attention to her phone conversation, but without the other half of the dialogue, their eavesdropping was pointless.

"Hello, David. What's up?"

"Yes."

"I'm sure I can. Why?"

"Do you really think so?"

"Yes. I'll call him immediately. Can he email it to you?"

"Okay, I'll let you know when to expect it."

As soon as Allison ended the call, Jack and Silvia fired questions at her.

"It could be a lead," she answered. "David wants a copy of my grandfather's will. Please forgive me, everyone, but I need to call my attorney," Allison apologized. "I don't want Jack's party interrupted by phone calls, so I need to take care of this now."

As the car made its way to Long Island, the passengers whispered excitedly, recalling the morning's event and prompting Zavie and Roberta to share details about their trip to Jamaica.

When they arrived, Wellington Manor would be abuzz with final preparations, not only for the party but for a houseful of overnight guests. Allison had instructed Martha to hire whatever help was needed for the weekend. The florists had delivered a van full of white flowers in mixed varieties. They were adorned with shiny silver bows and lush greenery. As Theo and James directed the decorators to add their final touches, Martha had the kitchen team well in-hand and Gretchen was in charge of the upstairs staff.

Once the guests were settled in their rooms and freshened up, a light lunch would be served in the conservatory. The caterers were due to arrive at four p.m., and the remaining guests should come around seven. In the front drawing room, Theo and James had the furniture artfully rearranged and the mammoth Persian rug removed to allow for dancing. The DJ would set up in the foyer, encouraging dancers to spill onto the marble floor. All of the home's French doors would remain open, encouraging party guests to flow freely from one room to another.

Less than twenty minutes later, Allison's phone vibrated again, interrupting her reverie. Embarrassed to be the cause of further interruptions, she turned toward the window, speaking in hushed tones to David Strong.

"I can't believe it," Allison said upon ending the phone call. She was more stunned than excited.

"What is it?" Jack asked. "Is there news about Marc?" He turned to face her squarely.

"All this time..." she began, staring into space. "All this time, he might have been right here in the city. We could have been together." She sought solace in Jack's comforting eyes. The other passengers abruptly ended their conversations and turned their attention to the couple.

"Where? Where in the city? The Morrison Home?" he asked, holding Allison's shoulders tenderly. Allie was aware of the electric—almost psychic—connection that radiated between her and Jack. There was obvious sexual energy, but so much more. Silvia must have noticed it, too because Allie heard her whisper to Edward, "These two belong together."

"It was just as David suspected," Allie said. "Opa established a charitable endowment the same year that Marc was taken away. The Morrison Home is one of its half dozen recipients and has been for over twenty years."

"But I thought you checked it out and no one by his name lived there," Jack said.

"Exactly. My mother was right. Opa had Marc's name changed when he was transferred from the Caring Cottage, or at least, David is pretty sure that's the case."

"But how can he prove it?" Silvia asked. "Didn't you say the records were probably sealed?"

"He's working with an attorney on obtaining a subpoena. If he can find evidence that Marc was kidnapped from my parents, the subpoena won't be a problem."

"But how can he prove it was a kidnapping?" asks Jack. "Wouldn't he need a witness? You were just a toddler and your parents…"

"Martha!" Allison and Jack said in unison.

"Of course, there's my mother's letter, too. David has a copy," Allison added. "I don't know if it'll stand up in court, but it certainly shows she didn't willingly give up her son." As the limo passed through the front gate of Wellington Manor, she said, "Gretchen will show you to your rooms where you can freshen up before lunch. Don't worry about your bags. Clarence and Felix will deliver them to you shortly. I can't wait to see what Theo and James have done. I put them in charge of the decorations."

Even before the group climbed the steps of the front portico, the massive wooden doors swung open to reveal Theo and James who were waiting to greet them.

"Okay, everyone!" James announced. "Close your eyes. I want you to experience the full impact all at once." He and Theo held the doors closed behind them.

"Do you mind if we climb the steps first?" Allie asked, teasing him.

"Of course not," Theo said, taking her arm on one side and Silvia's on the other. "Don't mind James. He's a little excited. Everything turned out perfectly and he wants you to love it."

"I'm sure it's beautiful. Now let's get our guests in out of the cold."

"Okay, gather around, close your eyes, and we'll open the doors on the count of three: one, two, three, open," James commanded, sweeping his arms flamboyantly.

After an initial silent pause, a collective gasp came from the crowd, followed by exclamations of "Oh my!" "Wow!" "Amazing!" all uttered at once. Standing in the massive foyer, the guests began slowly spinning in circles, trying to take in the scene before them.

Throughout the manor, tiny white lights twinkled among artfully placed, lush topiaries and potted evergreens. Garlands of fresh, fragrant running cedar, intertwined with white and silver ribbon, spilled down the banisters like ski slopes winding down a mountainside. Sparkling glass icicles hung from the chandeliers and sconces. Resembling snow drifts of varying heights, huge floral arrangements in white with silver-and-white bows adorned every available surface. Flanking the staircase were two long tables covered to the floor with delicate white fabric interwoven with silver threads. One table held a carefully constructed pyramid of champagne glasses. The other was set up to serve as the DJ's station. While the overall effect was that of a frozen wonderland, the transformation actually added warmth to Allison's childhood home. She could hardly wait to see it after dark when candlelight would further enhance the charm.

"Oh, James, Theo," Allison said. "You have outdone yourselves. It is absolutely stunning. Isn't it stunning, Jack? What do you think?"

"I'm blown away! All this for me? Thank you!"

"Allie said to pull out all the stops, so we did."

"You certainly did." Then, turning to Allie, Jack took her hands in his, kissed them, and looked into her eyes. "Thank you, Allie," he said quietly. "I feel so honored."

"That's exactly how I hoped you'd feel. Now let's get everyone's coats and prepare for an evening of celebration. Dr. Sanderling has arrived, and there's much more to come."

As Martha and Gretchen took the guests' coats, Martha announced that lunch was waiting in the conservatory.

"I don't know about everyone else," Allie said, "but I'm starved. Shall we eat before settling into our rooms?"

The response was a unanimous "yes!"

CHAPTER 47

The party was already underway when Allison appeared at the upstairs landing. More text messages and phone calls from David Strong delayed her entrance, but she was determined to keep his latest news to herself until after the party. She chose to wear a Giorgio Armani dress this evening. A full length in silver lamé from the previous year's fall collection, it was sleek and elegant in a design that elongated her petite figure. Simple silver earrings by Cartier hung beneath a stylish up-do, and strappy stiletto heels completed the impeccable ensemble. Allie's eyes lit up at the sight of Jack waiting at the bottom of the staircase in his rented tuxedo. For a few moments, as Allie descended the stairs to meet his outstretched hand, time stood still and only the two of them existed in the entire universe.

"You look delicious!" Jack said. He took her arm and tucked it gently in the crook of his elbow.

"And you look very handsome, Dr. Sanderling," she said, feeling a bit like a giddy teenager ready for the prom. "Now, how about introducing me to your friends?"

"With pleasure, Ms. Harmon! May I get you some champagne?"

"Yes, please."

They approached the sparkling glass-tower where a hired server handed each of them a glass of bubbly champagne. Then, as they mingled among the guests, Jack introduced Allie to his friends and colleagues. As the evening progressed, Allie was delighted to observe that Jack and his guests seemed to be enjoying themselves. By opening all of the French doors and creating multiple inviting groupings of furniture, Theo and James successfully accomplished the desired flow throughout the mansion. The DJ was excellent, offering a wide variety of music to encourage both dancing and conversation. The catered food was outstanding, and the wait staff circulated unobtrusively, keeping glasses and plates filled. Despite Allie's policy of concluding alcohol service at nine p.m.—a safety precaution inherited from her father—no one seemed anxious to leave even when the clock struck ten.

Allie asked the DJ to stop the music and direct everyone's attention to her as she stood on the third step of the staircase. As the guests turned their focus to her, she offered a toast to the new doctor. "Ladies and gentlemen, thank you for coming tonight and helping me honor Jack. Earning a PhD is no small accomplishment, and Jack has worked very hard to fulfill his dream. Please join me in toasting Doctor Jack Sanderling." She raised her glass and the guests followed. "To Jack," she said.

"To Jack," the guests responded in unison. Jack joined his host on the stairs and placed one arm around her waist. He acknowledged the group with a slight bow and responded with his own toast.

"Everyone here has played a part in the accomplishment of my goal. Thank you for your support, and thank you for being here tonight to help me celebrate. I'd like to propose a toast to our wonderful hostess. To Allie."

"To Allie."

"Thank you," she said. "And now I invite you to enjoy coffee and dessert and—"

Suddenly the magical evening turned form celebration to nightmare when Gretchen rushed from the kitchen, alarm lacing her voice.

"Miss Allison, come quickly! Please," she shouted. Immediately Allison knew something serious had happened. Otherwise, her well-trained staff would never consider interrupting a gathering, whether social or business. *Has a fire broken out in the kitchen? Is someone injured?* Allison began to imagine any number of horrible scenarios.

"Gretchen, what is it? What's happened?" she asked, noticing the color had drained from the woman's face.

"I'm sorry to interrupt, but you need to come! It's Martha! Please hurry!"

As Allie quickly followed Gretchen to the kitchen, the guests froze in place like statues in a wax museum. "Martha?" Allison asked. "What's happened?"

In the kitchen Martha was lying on the floor, motionless. One of the caterer's employees was administering CPR. "Oh, my God! Somebody call 911. Hurry!"

Allison knelt beside the lifeless woman, not sure what to do. Martha's face was a ghastly shade of gray. Allison had seen this color before. It was the unmistakable pallor of human death. She buried her face in her hands, trying to deny what was happening before her.

"Oh, Martha, please... come back. Please don't leave me. Where's that ambulance? Did somebody call an ambulance?"

"Yes, Miss, it's on its way," a faceless voice said.

"What happened? How did this happen?" Allison said, not actually caring about the how or what, but needing to do or say something, anything, to make sense of the surreal scene before her. Jack knelt beside Allie, placing an arm around her.

"She just collapsed, Miss," Gretchen said, crying. "She wasn't breathing. One minute she was fine and the next... I don't know... where's that ambulance?" She rushed to the window to check. "They're here," she said. "They're coming through the gate now!"

"Please, hurry," Allison whispered helplessly, sensing there was no hope. "Oh, Jack, I think she's gone." She sobbed into his shoulder.

The next few minutes produced a flurry of activity as the paramedics entered and took over the resuscitation efforts. In a matter of minutes the cheerful atmosphere of a perfect party had undergone a terrible transformation. Someone ushered the guests out of the kitchen to wait in other rooms.

As the paramedics applied paddles to Martha's chest and repeatedly shocked her heart, time seemed to slow and then stop. Allie knew, but couldn't accept, that her beloved Martha was dead. How can this be? Was Martha showing signs of stress that Allie missed? Did she have a heart attack? Had Allie been working her too hard? Was the party too much for her? Allie couldn't help but feel responsible, but the worst part of this nightmarish ending to a beautiful evening happened just before she came downstairs. Allie had talked to David Strong once again. He told her he was certain her brother lived at Morrison Home, and he would go there with a subpoena first thing Monday morning. All those years, Martha had waited and hoped to be reunited with Marc, and now within days of his discovery, she was gone.

Finally the paramedic had no recourse but to pronounce Martha dead, and Allie rushed to the lifeless body. Cradling Martha in her arms, the tears flowed until Jack gently helped her release Martha's soulless form.

"I need to speak to our guests," she said quietly, still dazed.

"I'll do it," Jack offered. "You stay here until they've gone."

"But…"

"Stay here. I'll take care of it," he repeated. Too weak to resist, Allie acquiesced.

"Come on, Miss," Gretchen said, helping her up with one hand while, with the other, attempting unsuccessfully to stem her own flow of tears. "Let's go to Martha's apartment where you can lie down."

"Wait," Allie said, remembering something. She knelt beside the body once more and carefully removed the gold brooch from Martha's collar. She had not seen Martha's uniform without it since the day she received it in the hospital—Christmas Day.

CHAPTER 48

By the time Jack finished explaining the situation to some fifty subdued party guests and bid them all "good-night," Allie managed to pull herself together. Jack found her sitting alone in Martha's apartment. Although Gretchen hesitated to leave her, Allie insisted she go home to her own family and get some rest. By eleven thirty, the ambulance and the caterer had departed and the overnight invitees were tucked into their rooms for the night. Clarence locked all the outside doors and trudged along the icy, but familiar, path to his cottage.

Jack knocked gently on the apartment door and entered without waiting for an answer. Allie, who had been sitting in near darkness, looked up with vacant eyes. Occupying Martha's favorite rocking chair beside the cold fireplace, she had been fingering the brooch and recalling memories of special times she had shared with her surrogate mother through the years. A relationship complicated by the employer-employee status, it endured all those years because of an underlying—but mostly unspoken—love between the two women.

Jack sat on the floor and rested his head on her lap. "Are you okay?"

"I'll be fine," she said, stroking his thick hair. "You must be tired. Why don't you go to bed and I'll see you in the morning. Has everyone left?"

"Hm-hm. Well, except the ones who are spending the night." He yawned. "It was a wonderful party, Allie. Thanks."

"Yeah, right up until the dramatic finale. Jack, I'm afraid I killed Martha."

"What? You're joking, right?" he asked, incredulous.

"What if she died because I worked her too hard? She wasn't a young woman, you know. Maybe she shouldn't have been working at all."

"Don't be ridiculous! From what I've seen, you couldn't have stopped her. She seemed to really enjoy her work, and she was excited about the party. Listen, Allie, let's not go assigning blame, at least not before hearing the coroner's report."

"You're right, of course, but I feel responsible somehow. You go to bed. I think I'll sleep in Martha's bed tonight. She used to let me sleep with her sometimes when I was little, especially right after her family died."

"I want to be with you tonight, Allie."

"Oh, Jack, you know I adore you, and there's nothing I'd like more, but this isn't the right time."

"I'm not talking about sex. As much as I want to take that step, I'd never take advantage of your grief. Do you trust me?"

"Of course, but I'm feeling very vulnerable right now. I'm not sure I can trust *myself*. It's just that I want our first time to be, well... planned and... special."

"I understand."

"You do?"

"I may have to sit on my hands all night, but I understand."

"I love you, Jack Sanderling." She looked deeply into his hypnotic blue eyes. He took her hands in his, gently pulled her out of the chair, and led her to the sofa.

"And I love you, Allison Harmon." He held her face and kissed her forehead. "Don't make me wait too long to show you just how much," he said, pulling one of Martha's colorful afghans across their laps. "Now, let's get some sleep." Allie switched off the table lamp and rested her head on Jack's shoulder, at once realizing how very tired she was and how grateful she was to have this amazing man in her life.

CHAPTER 49

The next morning, Silvia was the first to rise. Descending the staircase, she was struck by the sad realization that no aroma of freshly baked cinnamon rolls would awaken the household this morning. She crossed the marble foyer which had been denuded of all signs of last evening's revelry and discovered that Gretchen already prepared coffee and was bustling about in the kitchen.

"Good morning, Mrs. Sanderling. I hope you slept well," Gretchen said, obviously trying to sound chipper. Silvia noticed that Gretchen's eyes were swollen and rimmed with dark circles.

"Gretchen, you must be exhausted. Here, let me help with breakfast."

"No, no, Ma'am. Please have some coffee and relax. I'll have breakfast ready in a jiffy. I'm afraid I got a late start this morning," she said apologetically.

"Of course you did, you poor thing. Did you get any sleep at all?" Silvia asked.

"A couple hours. I'll be fine."

"Listen, Honey, I'm not used to being idle and I'd really like to help. What are we making?"

"I thought we'd have pancakes and sausage. How does that sound?"

"Perfect. Where's the griddle?"

Despite Gretchen's obvious discomfort at allowing a house guest to work alongside her in the kitchen, she looked relieved and grateful for the help. Given the scene that transpired in this very kitchen last night, she probably appreciated the distracting conversation. Within thirty minutes, Silvia learned a good deal about Gretchen's husband and children, and the pair whipped up enough scrambled eggs, pancakes, and sausages to feed all of the blurry-eyed zombies that gradually appeared throughout the morning. Soon, Zavie and Roberta, followed by Simon and Carolyn, entered the dining room to find a mouth-watering feast—including fresh orange juice and warm maple syrup—waiting in chafing dishes on the sideboard. Lastly, Edward arrived and they all unreservedly filled their plates. Silvia was glaringly aware of the only two absentees. *Where are Jack and Allie?* Earlier, Silvia noticed that both bedroom doors were open when she passed by them. The beds were turned down, but clearly hadn't been slept in. She had expected to find the pair downstairs, but by nine a.m., they still hadn't made an appearance.

Finally, at 9:20, Jack entered the dining room through the kitchen door, looking like something the cat ate and regurgitated. Wearing the same, yet rumpled, tuxedo from the night before, minus shoes, his five o'clock shadow had bourgeoned into a beard and his eyes were bloodshot. Passing through the kitchen, he asked Gretchen to attend to Allie, who wanted to freshen up before greeting her guests.

"Whoa, Dude! What happened to you?" Zavie said, looking up from his pancakes.

"Well, good morning, sunshine," Silvia said. "Where did you crash last night?"

"Hm, coffee first, questions later," Jack mumbled, padding to the sideboard. During her visit, Silvia had become increasingly aware that Jack's relationship with Allie was growing serious, and now her imagination was working overtime. She decided not to embarrass her son by continuing the inquisition.

Allie climbed the back stairs to her room, blessed coffee in hand. Her neck was stiff from sleeping on Jack's shoulder all night, and she was anxious to let a steamy shower soothe her body aches as it washed away the ache in her heart. Last night seemed like a bad dream. Could Martha really be gone? The woman had always been a part of her life, but surely Allie realized Martha couldn't live forever.

As the caffeine awakened her and the hot shower eased her tight muscles, myriad details flooded her mind. Funeral arrangements must be made first thing Monday. But she wanted to accompany Mr. Strong to the Morrison Home on Monday morning. She had already postponed a ten a.m. business meeting that had been set since before Christmas, and she's so far behind at work that it'll take weeks of overtime to catch up. Then, she needed to find a new housekeeper, or should she put Wellington up for sale? What will happen to Gretchen, Felix, and Clarence if she sold it? And what about her promise to Jack that they would discuss their future together? As the CEO of a major company, Allie was accustomed to keeping many plates spinning at once, but at that moment, she was overwhelmed and on the verge of collapse. Giving in to stress and grief, she indulged in a good cry, trusting the running water to mask her sobs.

By the time Allie descended the stairs, she managed to pull herself together, emotionally and physically. She found the women talking in the conservatory. Silvia stood and greeted her with a hug. "How are you, Sweetie? What a night! You must be worn out."

"I'm okay, but I apologize for not joining you for breakfast." Then turning to Roberta and Carolyn, Allie said, "Good morning, ladies. Where are the men?"

"Edward is devouring your father's library, and the others are taking advantage of your exercise equipment," Silvia explained.

"Oh, good. I'm glad you all are making yourselves at home. I'm afraid I haven't been a very attentive host."

"You've been a wonderful host, and Gretchen has taken very good care of us this morning. Would you like some coffee? She just brought a fresh pot."

"Absolutely, and keep it coming." Allie curled up in one of the Papasan chairs. "Well, that was quite an evening, wasn't it?" she said sarcastically.

"The party was wonderful," Roberta said. "You had no control over what happened at the end."

"I know, but I regret the timing of it. I wanted Jack's celebration to be special."

"Honey, it was magical," Silvia said. "You couldn't have done anything more to make it a memorable occasion."

"I agree," Carolyn said. "Now tell us what we can do to help you through the next few days."

"You're doing it," Allie said. "I'm so glad you're here."

CHAPTER 50

The next few days produced a flurry of activity. Ever since the ambulance was summoned to Wellington Manor Saturday night, reporters were gathered outside the gates. Allison hired extra security services to cover both of her residences, as well as H & H headquarters. Fortunately, Simon and Carolyn escaped, undetected, Tuesday night to catch their flight home, but Allie knew the others must feel like they were being held prisoner in a very luxurious penitentiary. Even Gretchen camped out for the week, fearing the paparazzi would follow her home. With much false speculation being reported about what happened at the Harmon estate, Allison called a press conference. She hoped that, by giving the press a story, her remaining guests would be able to leave without being hounded or followed.

Once again, Allison had to delay the process of finding her brother, but after his visit to the Morrison Home, Strong called her with good news. The subpoena held up in court, requiring the administration to give him access to the records of the two male residents who could possibly turn out to be Marc. Despite Allison's eagerness to reveal the truth about her brother, she insisted that

David wait until she can accompany him... Friday at the earliest. Of course, she wanted Jack there, as well.

With the help of Silvia and Theo, Allison planned a fitting memorial service for Martha, and with the help of Theo's Facebook and Twitter skills, Martha's few remaining relatives were summoned in time to attend. It turned out that Martha was active in a women's club at her small Catholic church in the Bronx. Allie knew Martha had grown up in the Bronx, but she was embarrassed to admit she didn't know about the club or about Martha's continued involvement there. Like her father, Allison made it a policy not to pry into her employees' personal affairs or ask about their days off. It was her father's way of maintaining a "professional distance." But now she wondered if she should have shown more interest in Martha's private life.

According to Martha's wishes, Allison arranged for a Mass at Martha's church and, upon departing for the funeral, was relieved to find the reporters had disbanded. After the Mass, a lovely reception was held in the parish hall, prepared by the women's club. Allie felt like an outsider, an intruder into Martha's *real* life. For the first time, she found herself questioning one of her father's business practices and made a mental note to examine other policies she had always taken for granted.

As a child, Allie wasn't allowed to attend the funerals for Martha's husband and son, so she didn't even know where they were laid to rest—until now. Adjacent to the church was a peaceful memorial garden, where a small family plot awaited Martha's remains. She would rest in peace beside her husband, Gerald, and son, Martin.

As the limousine pulled away, Allie dissolved into tears once more, realizing that both Wellington Manor and her life are forever changed by Martha's passing. Once again, Jack was there to comfort and give her strength. As she allowed him to wrap her in his sturdy embrace, her heart burst with love for him.

Chapter 51

It was time for Silvia to go home to Virginia. Leaving her sons was always difficult, but this visit produced an unforeseen, and equally tough, separation. She had no other choice, of course, but thoughts of leaving Edward were filling her with angst. As the limo pulled into Penn Station, she began the arduous task of saying good-bye to Zavie, who was like her third son, and Roberta, who had won her heart—and her approval—in just a few short days. Then she turned to Jack, her eyes glistening with mother-love. "I'm so proud of you, son," she said, trying to keep herself from a total meltdown.

"Thanks, Mom, and thanks for being here." He gave her a big hug.

"Honey, I wouldn't have missed it." Then, turning to Allie, but still addressing Jack, she added, "I think you have exquisite taste in women. Thank you, Allie, for opening your beautiful home to all of us and for making my son happier than I've seen him in many years."

"Oh, Silvia, I don't want you to go." Allie wrapped her in a warm embrace. "I—" But before she could continue, Silvia cut her off.

"Now, now, enough of this sentimental foolishness," she said, stiffening in an effort to regain control of her emotions. "If we keep this up, I'll have to completely re-do my makeup. Come on, Edward, how about walking me to the gate?"

"With pleasure, my dear." He helped her out of the car where Felix waited with her suitcases. "Please don't wait," he called back to the others. "I can take a taxi home."

"Absolutely not," Allie said. "Take your time. We'll be right here."

Edward started to argue, but then complied. "You're very kind. I won't be long."

A few minutes later, as Silvia settled into her seat on the train, she admitted to herself that she had fallen in love with Professor Hastings, a man she had known for only two weeks. He declared his love for her, as well, and his goodbye kiss convinced her that his declaration was, indeed, genuine. Feeling thrilled, confused, sad, and happy all at once, she decided a good, long nap was in order.

CHAPTER 52

Finally Allison was able to spend a full day at the office, but her mind was not on her work, and because sleep eluded her the night before, she dragged through the day. Mr. Strong had made an appointment to visit the Morrison Home. Of course, Allison invited Jack to accompany her, and they made plans to meet for breakfast the next morning. Allison wanted to ensure there would be no reporters on the scene, so she took a taxi to the restaurant. From there, Strong was scheduled to pick them up at nine thirty and, hopefully by ten a.m., Allison would meet her brother.

"Oh, Jack! I'm so excited and so scared," Allie said as they slid into an out-of-the-way booth. "I ordered all this food, but I don't think I can eat anything."

"I can understand excitement, but what are you scared about?" he asked, chomping on a bagel slathered in cream cheese.

"What if David is wrong and Marc isn't at the Morrison Home, after all?"

"Then we'll keep looking until we find him."

"What if we find Marc and he doesn't want to have anything to do with me?"

"He's going to love you just like I do, and besides, we'll take it slow, let him get used to us and get to know us."

"You're right. I'm just being a worry wart."

"What is a worry wart, anyway?"

"My father used to call me a worry wart when I was little. I thought it was because I worried about him being alone and always tried to take care of him. So, I got in the habit of calling him a worry wart whenever he was stressed about something at work. Later, I discovered he was actually calling me a pest."

"A pest? How did you know?"

"Once when I was a teenager, I was badgering him to let me skip school and go with him on a business trip. I worried him to death about it for days and he called me his 'little worry wart.' That's when I got the connection."

They laughed, and Allie relaxed a bit.

"Jack, do you think Marc would want to come and live with us? Oh, I guess I should ask you first. How would you feel about that?"

"What makes you think *I* want to live with us?" he teased.

"But I thought…" Allie stammered. Her coffee cup stopped halfway to her mouth and her eyes met his with such a pained look that he immediately apologized.

"Babe, I'm sorry! I'm just playing with you, trying to get you to chill out." He reached for her hand. "You know I want us to be together, and I want your brother to be a part of our family, but you need to remember he has lived at the Morrison Home for many years. It's probably the only home he remembers, and it might be upsetting to take him away from everything and everyone he has ever known. We don't even know how independent he is or how much care he might require."

"Yes, of course, but I could offer him so much."

"Let's take it one step at a time, okay? First, we need to find him."

Allie took another sip of coffee and sank back into the booth, finally relaxing her tense shoulders. "I'm glad you're coming with us. Thank you for supporting me in this."

"I just want you to be happy and I want to marry you, Allie. Will you marry me?"

"Whoa, what happened to taking things one step at a time?"

"Oh. Right."

"Allie, will you think about marrying me?"

"Yes I will." She giggled.

Soon they were headed to a residential area in Queens and, a few minutes before ten, David, who had talked non-stop since picking them up, pulled into the driveway of the Morrison Home. Allie was surprised to find it looked like an ordinary house. She had expected it to resemble a nursing home or some sterile medical facility. As Jack helped her out of the car, she was shaking.

"I'm so nervous," she said. "But it's beautiful. Even in the dead of winter, it's beautiful."

"This is one of the best facilities in the state." David joined them on the sidewalk.

"Well, I guess I have to give Opa credit for that," Allie said. "He always did have impeccable taste."

"Shall we go in?" David asked, motioning to the front steps.

"Come on, Allie. I'll be right beside you the whole time," Jack said.

Allie straightened, took a deep breath of cold air, and with false bravado, proclaimed, "Okay, I'm ready."

The trio was greeted at the front door by a friendly young man who ushered them into a pleasant living room. His name tag said, "Hello, my name is Miguel."

"Hi, I'm Miguel, one of the volunteers here. Are you expected?"

"Yes," David said. "We have an appointment to see the director, Ms. Chadwick. My name is David Strong and this is my client, Allison Harmon and—"

"Allison Harmon! Theeee Allison Harmon? Yes, you are! Dios Mio! I've seen you on TV!"

"Please, Miguel, don't make a fuss," Allison said, embarrassed. "We don't want to be disruptive. Could you please just tell Ms. Chadwick we're here?"

"Si, yes, I'll get her. Please be seated," he said. Then, walking away, he muttered to himself, excitedly, in Spanish.

As they waited in the comfortable overstuffed furniture, they heard voices coming from a room at the rear of the house. The muffled sounds of men's voices were mixed with bouncing ping pong balls, intermittent applause, laughter and exclamations of "Good job! Atta boy! You got this!"

"It sounds like they're having fun," Allie said. "Oh, Jack, this place seems so warm and inviting. I was expecting…"

A tall, attractive, middle-aged woman entered the room and greeted them. Jack and David stood. "Hi, I'm Helen Chadwick," she said, shaking their hands. "Ms. Harmon, you seem to have charmed Miguel. I'm not sure he'll ever recover."

"I'm sorry about that, Ms. Chadwick. I really don't want to create any problems."

"No, no don't worry. You made his day, and call me Helen." Then, turning to David, she said, "You must be David Strong. We talked on the phone. And who's this?"

Allison realized, for the first time, that she didn't quite know how to introduce Jack. "This is Jack Sanderling, my... uh, my friend."

"Well, I understand you've come with a subpoena, David. Please, follow me and we'll get down to business." She walked them down a long hallway, past two small offices and a restroom. At the end of the hall, they entered her large, pleasant, sunny office where she invited them to be seated in leather chairs.

"What a gorgeous facility." Allison looked about the room. "It seems like a very well-maintained Victorian home. It has been beautifully restored."

"Yes, the Mellon Foundation is responsible for its original restoration, but the families of our clients pay a great deal to keep their young men here."

"How many are living here?" Jack asked.

"We're set up to house fifteen, but right now we have fourteen. Most of them have lived here their entire lives." Turning to David, she asked, "Would you mind if we get started? I'm afraid I have another appointment at eleven."

"Actually, Helen," Allison said, "would you mind if I looked around while you and David handle the legal issues? I'd love to see the rest of the facility."

"That's not a problem. We have an open-door policy. The only thing we ask is that you not enter the bedrooms upstairs without a staff member to escort you."

"Thank you." Allie took Jack's hand and eagerly pulled him out the door. Once out of ear-shot, Allie said, "Jack, I'm sure he's here. I just feel it. I'm going to meet my brother today."

Jack offered the voice of reason. "Don't get ahead of yourself, Allie. Let's wait to see what David finds out."

"Come on," she said, ignoring his cautionary advice. "Let's see what all the excitement is about."

They headed toward the source of the flurry and discover a large recreation room, abuzz with activity. At one end were two ping pong tables, where young men played quite adeptly despite their obvious limitations. Numerous staff members and volunteers cheered them on.

The other end of the long room was set up with round tables and chairs flanked by a whole wall of games, puzzles, and Legos stored neatly in labeled baskets. In the center of the wall was a large, flat-screen TV that could be viewed from comfortable looking chairs that divided the room. French doors led out to a patio and a brick walled back yard that, although unusable this time of year, undoubtedly provided welcome outdoor space during New York's short-lived warmer months. Allison visually isolated the young men with Down syndrome. She studied each one carefully, trying to discern their ages. Finally, she narrowed the group down to three men she thought could be in their mid-twenties. One, who was referred to as Alex, played ping pong. Another was working a puzzle with a staff member, and the third was playing checkers with Miguel.

Everyone was getting individual attention. It seemed there were as many staff members as there were residents. Allison left Jack watching the table tennis match and sidled up to the puzzle table. "Hi, my name's Allison," she said. What's yours?"

"This is George," the woman offered. "...and I'm Trina," she added, turning her name tag so Allison could see it. "George is non-verbal, but he's a whiz at puzzles." George slapped a puzzle piece into place and laughed uproariously. "Very good, George!" Trina said. "He has done this same puzzle at least a hundred times, but every time is like the first."

"I can see that," Allison said, smiling at George's obvious pride. "How old is George, Trina?"

"I think he's around thirty. Let's see. He came here nine years ago when his mother died. He had just turned twenty-one, so..." Trina laid down a puzzle piece and quickly counted on her fingers. "Yup, thirty."

"Well it was nice to meet you, Trina. So long, George!"

"George, can you wave good-bye?" Trina prompted. Without looking up, he waved, and Allie moved on to the checkers table.

"Hi, my name's Allison. Who is this clever young man?" she asked, noticing he had just jumped two of his opponent's checkers. Suddenly, Miguel, who had his back turned to her, jumped up, nearly upending the table. "Ms. Harmon, it's you," he said, flustered.

"Timmy, this is a famous lady: Allison Harmon!"

"Hi, Aysin Harmon! You yike to pay checkers?" Timmy asked.

"Hi, Timmy. Yes, I do. My father and I used to play all the time."

"Please sit down, Ms. Harmon." Miguel pointed to a vacant chair opposite his.

"Thank you... and you sit down, too, Miguel. I didn't mean to interrupt your game."

"It's okay. Timmy always beats me, so I'm glad for the interruption."

"Timmy ahways beats Miguay!" Timmy parroted, laughing and thumping his chest.

"Say, can I get you something to drink?" Miguel asked. "We have lemonade and iced tea in the dining room."

"Actually, I'd love a glass of water. Thanks."

Allie was not thirsty, but she wanted the chance to talk to Timmy alone. There was something about this young man that rang familiar. She felt an instant connection. Maybe it was the eyes that, although set in the characteristic epicanthic fold, were the same brown as her own. Her heart felt like it would pound out of her chest, but she had to be careful to hide her suspicion until she knew for sure.

"You want to pay?" Timmy asked.

"Yes, I'd love to."

"Timmy yikes back, okay?"

"Oh, that's perfect, 'cause I like red."

As Timmy reset the board, Jack approached. "I see you have a new friend," he said.

"Jack, this is Timmy. Timmy, this is my friend, Jack."

"Hi, Jack! You yike to pay checkers?" With intense eyes, Allie tried to telegraph to Jack, "I think this is Marc." She was having a hard time restraining her excitement.

"I'm not very good. Why don't I just watch?"

"Okay." Timmy said.

"Timmy starts," he announced. *It's cute the way he refers to himself in the third person*, Allie thought.

They played silently for a minute or so, and then Allie asked, "Timmy, do you like living at the Morrison Home?"

"Timmy yikes Migu-ay and Ms. Hay-en and Marty and Trina and Freddie and… yots of friends."

"What else do you do besides play checkers?"

"Timmy woks."

"You have a job?" Jack asked.

"Timmy has job. Timmy woks in l-libary." This time he pronounced the 'l' sound deliberately, like he had practiced it.

"You do? Wow! That must be fun!" Allie said.

"Yeah. King me, Aysin!"

"You little sneak! How did you get there?"

"Ha, ha, ha!" Timmy's eyes twinkled as he roared with laughter. "Timmy ahways win checkers, right Miguay?"

"Si, amigo," Miguel, who had just returned from the dining room, agreed. He must have overheard the conversation and offered clarification on the job issue. "All of the residents have jobs here. It helps them learn important life skills and keeps them busy. Timmy knows his alphabet and numbers, so he works in the library, sorting books."

"Oh, so the library is here in the building?" Allison asked.

"Yes, most of these men are quite low functioning. They wouldn't be successful in the outside world. Timmy is probably the highest functioning of our residents."

"You want to see Timmy's l-libary, Aysin?" Timmy asked.

"Yes, I'd love to."

"Okay, Miguay? I show Aysin Timmy's libary? Jack, you come, too."

"Sure," Miguel said. "I'll go with you. Let me just tell the others where we're going."

Timmy, intent on showing the visitors where he worked, forgot all about the checkers game. As he stood, Allison noticed his short stature. After seeing him seated, she had expected him to be taller, but his limbs were out of proportion with his torso and he was no taller than she. He took her hand, gently, causing an electric current to surge through her entire body. *We know each other*, she thought with certainty. *This is my brother, Marc. I'm sure of it.*

Timmy proudly showed his guests the library, which was filled with children's books, magazines, and elementary textbooks. "Timmy does a great job, here," Miguel said. "He rarely makes a mistake."

"See, Aysin-Jack? Timmy's desk. Timmy's stamp pad. Timmy's job."

"I can see you're very conscientious about your work, Timmy."

"Very con, very con-si-en..." he tried to say.

"Conscientious. It means you do a good job," Allie said, tears starting to sting her eyes.

"Oh, yeah, Ms. Hay-en says Timmy does a good job," Timmy said with innocent pride.

"He's a total sweetheart, Jack," she whispered. "I could eat him up."

"Please, Allie, don't get your heart set just yet. He may not be..."

"You want to see my room, Aysin-Jack?" Allison adored the way Timmy ran their names together like they're one person. *How poignant that he knows Jack and I belong together,* she thought.

"Yes, we'd love to see your room. Is it okay, Miguel?"

"I'll have to get a staff member to accompany you. Rules, you know."

"Of course. We understand."

"Marty and Timmy share," Timmy said while they waited at the bottom of the stairs.

"Oh, you have a roommate?" Jack asked.

"Marty is Timmy's friend. Marty is Timmy's roommate."

"Will he mind if we go in his room?"

"No, Marty is Timmy's friend."

Entering the bedroom, Allie was struck by how clean and tidy it was. The beds were made and everything seemed to be in its proper place.

"I like your room, Timmy," Allison said. "Who keeps it so neat?"

"Timmy and Marty. We make our beds every day and put our dirty cothes in the hamper every day. Sometimes, the maids come."

"Well, you certainly do a good job."

"Marty helps. Marty is Timmy's friend."

"You seem to have lots of friends here, Timmy," Jack said.

"Yeah."

As Allie moved about the room, she noticed it was filled with vibrant colors, like a child's bedroom. The twin beds were covered with matching Spiderman bedspreads in red and blue. At the windows, cheerful red curtains coordinated with throw pillows on the beds and chairs. A collection of model cars was neatly displayed on the dresser. Helen and David appeared at the door. "There you are," David said. "We've been looking all over for you. I have some interesting news to share with…" Before he could finish, Allison dissolved into sobs.

"Allie, what is it?" Jack asked, rushing to her side.

"Aysin sad?" Timmy asked, looking very concerned. She was clutching something to her chest, something she found on Timmy's nightstand.

Timmy began patting her on the shoulder. "Don't cry, Aysin. Don't be sad, Aysin."

"Oh, Timmy—I'm not sad. I'm very, very happy!" She revealed her discovery: a framed photograph. "Look, Jack." It was identical to the photograph that her mother saved for her in the safe deposit box, the one where she was holding her baby brother.

"I don't need to hear your news, David. I've found my brother." Then addressing Timmy through her tears and pointing to the baby, she asked, "Do you know who this is?"

"Baby Timmy," he answered.

"And who is this?" she asked pointing to the little girl holding him.

"Sister," he answered.

"That's right. That's your sister, Allison. Timmy, I'm your sister."

Timmy, looking totally confused, studied the photo and then Allison.

"Okay now, Aysin?" he asked, still concerned about her crying.

"Yes, I'm okay now." She knew he didn't understand what was happening, but it didn't matter. She wanted to grab him and smother him in a giant hug, but she knew it would probably freak him out.

There would be time enough to help him get used to the idea. For now, all that mattered was that she found Marc.

David Strong lowered the file that he was about to show her. He looked like the wind had been let out of his sails... but in a good way.

"Oh, Jack! To think that Martha missed this by just a few days!" The waterworks started anew and Jack, seeing the concern return to Timmy's face, ushered Allie out of the room.

Back downstairs, Jack let her release every bit of her overflowing joy and grief onto his lapel. Finally, her shaking began to subside and she regained control. "I'm sorry. I know I shouldn't have fallen apart in front of Timmy. I just couldn't help it... and hearing the coroner's report yesterday was such a relief. A brain aneurism is not something I could have caused or prevented. It's all so much to absorb at once."

"I know, Babe. It's okay. You had about twenty-five years worth of tears stored up. It was a geyser that finally had to erupt." He stroked her hair and kissed the top of her head.

She looked up to meet his eyes. "Do you know how wonderful you are?"

"Oh, dear!" he said, pushing her away at arms' length. "You may not want to look in a mirror."

She knew her nose and eyes were beet red and black mascara was streaming down her cheeks. Jack had probably caressed her hair into a matted mess.

"This day has been totally worth a good 'ugly-cry,'" she said, "but I'd better go freshen up before I scare my brother any more than I have already."

CHAPTER 53

June 25, one year later

"Roberta, I thought this day would never come. I'm so happy I feel like I could fly!" Roberta helped Allie attach her one-of-a kind von Förstenberg wedding veil. Diane had always been Allie's favorite designer and one of her company's best costumers, so choosing her to design her gown and those of her attendants was a no-brainer. In their exquisite matching aqua gowns, Lydia and Lynette looked identical except for Lydia's baby bump.

"Just look at the rose garden," Allie exclaimed, pulling back the curtain and peering beyond the sparkling pool. "Could it be any more perfect? And the sun is actually shining. I was so worried it would rain."

"You need to stand still if you want me to finish this," Roberta said. "I feel like I'm trying to dress a dragonfly."

"I'm sorry. I'm a bundle of nervous energy. I hope Jack didn't get caught in traffic. What if they're late?" Jack and Zavie were in Queens to pick up Timmy. As much as Allie would have wanted Timmy to live with them, she had decided it would be too traumatic for him to leave the only home and friends he has ever known. She has visited him every week—sometimes twice a week—since discovering his whereabouts more than a year ago. He viewed her more as a special friend than a sister, but that was fine with her.

"Stop worrying. They'll be here on time," Roberta said.

"Oh, Roberta, I'm so glad to have you and Zavie here on our special day."

"Our best friends are getting married. Where else would we be? And besides, we've jumped on board the wedding express and it just keeps rollin' along."

"I know—can you believe it? First you and Zavie, then Silvia and Edward? It's like an epidemic. I wish Daddy could be here today. Then it really *would* be perfect. And Martha… Can you imagine how thrilled…" Her voice trailed off as she visualized both Martha and her father watching her marry her soul mate with her precious brother by her side. She let out a long sigh and began to tear up.

Roberta interrupted her reverie. "Honey, you'd better stop that or you're gonna' have to redo your makeup and mine, too."

"I could do without those incessant helicopters," Allie shouted, waving a fist at the roaring sky. "Can't we have just this one special day to ourselves?"

"It's the price you pay for fame, honey. You should see the crowd of reporters waiting outside the front gate."

"Well, they had better let my groom and his best man through the gate or there'll be hell to pay. Your wedding was so peaceful and private, Roberta. Maybe Jack and I should have eloped to Jamaica."

"Since you founded that orphanage in Kingston," Roberta said, "I predict that you and Jack will be taking many trips to the island."

"I hope so," Allie said. "I miss those precious children already."

Silvia entered the master suite—which Allie had finally claimed—looking beautiful in her new blue chiffon dress and strappy pumps. All the women had their hair and nails done earlier, and Silvia looked like a million bucks. Allie suspected she had never before permitted herself such a luxury.

"Oh, my dears… You look gorgeous, all of you," she said.

"Holy mother-of-the-groom," Roberta said. "You look like a movie star. That blue is definitely *your* color."

"You can say that again," Allie agreed, carefully drying her tears so as not to smudge her mascara. "Any sign of the groom yet?"

"Actually, he just texted me to let you know they're down the street trying to shove their way through the traffic jam, and Theo sends word that everything is set and on schedule."

"Okay, I guess this is it, then. In less than an hour, I'll be Mrs. Jack Sanderling."

As the guests began to arrive, they were ushered to some two hundred white folding chairs that were carefully positioned on the lawn and connected by yards of flowing white ribbon. The sounds of string quartet music wafted through the open window from the garden below. James had erected a flower covered arch at the far end of the rose garden to function as a focal point for the ceremony.

"Before you go downstairs, I want to give you something," Silvia said, revealing a small box she had been holding behind her back. "My mother gave me a string of pearls that had been my grandmother's for my first wedding." She opened the box to reveal a delicate gold chain, adorned with three pearls and matching pearl earrings. "When I realized I wasn't going to have any daughters of my own, I had her strand of pearls made into two sets for my future daughters-in-law. You don't have to wear them today, but I want you to have them now on the day that you marry my son."

"Oh, Silvia! Of course I'll wear them today. They're beautiful and I am so honored. Thank you." Allie kissed her and proceeded to remove the earrings that she had originally planned to wear. "I can wear these on my honeymoon," she said, laying them on the dresser.

Roberta lifted Allie's veil to make way for the necklace exchange. "Here girl, let me help you. I think it's so romantic that you and Jack are going back to Paris for your honeymoon."

"I just hope we aren't hounded by reporters the whole time," Allie said, and then turning to face Silvia, added, "and I hope your son realizes what he's getting himself into."

"Honey, my son, the new head curator," she said, "would follow you into a fiery furnace, if necessary!"

"What an amazing son you raised, Mrs. Hastings."
"Oh, now that sounds real fine," she said, her southern accent drawing out the word so it sounded like 'fah-n'. "I'm still getting used to my new name, but I must say, I like it, and I actually like living here. I never saw myself leaving Bedford, but you've made the transition so smooth, Allie. Thank you for opening your beautiful home to us."

"It's your home now, too... *Mom*... and I love having life and energy restored to this old house. Besides, whenever we get tired of each other, you and Edward can escape to his apartment and Jack and I can retreat to my—our—condo."

"But first, ladies," Roberta said, "If I may interrupt this mutual admiration society, we have a wedding to attend."

The recipe for

MARTHA'S MOUTHWATERING CINNAMON BUNS

follows on the next page.

MARTHA'S MOUTHWATERING CINNAMON BUNS

Preheat oven to 400 degrees.

Bun Ingredients:
½ c. milk
4 c. sifted flour
1 yeast cake or 1 pkg. dried yeast
¼ c. margarine
¾ tsp. salt
1 egg, beaten
1/3 c. granulated sugar
1 c. brown sugar
¼ c. chopped pecans
3 tbs. melted butter
Ground cinnamon

Dissolve yeast in lukewarm water. Scald milk. Add granulated sugar, salt and shortening to scalded milk. Stir until sugar is dissolved. When milk has cooled to lukewarm, add yeast and beaten egg. Mix thoroughly.

Gradually add flour, beating well. Knead lightly, working in enough flour to make dough workable. Place dough in a greased bowl; cover and let stand in a warm place. Let rise about 2 hours. Dough should double in size.

Remove dough to a floured board. Roll into a rectangle about 1/4" thick. Brush with melted butter. Sprinkle with cinnamon, brown sugar and pecans.

Roll dough from long side to opposite side. With a serrated knife, cut slices ½" thick. Place slices on a greased cookie sheet. Let rise in a warm place (about 1 hour).

Bake at 400 degrees for 20 – 25 minutes.

Let cool on wire rack, enough to apply icing.

Icing ingredients:
1/3 c. softened butter
¼ tsp. salt
1 tsp. vanilla extract
1 lb. sifted confectioners' sugar
¼ c. milk (approximate)

Cream butter, salt and vanilla until light and fluffy. Add sugar gradually, beating well after each addition. Add milk until smooth and of spreading consistency. Spread on warm cinnamon buns and serve immediately.

ABOUT THE AUTHOR

After forty-five years as an educator and musician, Cindy L. Freeman began writing fiction. She relishes a good mystery, as in her novella, *Diary in the Attic* or an intriguing family secret, as in her novel, *Unrevealed* . In 2012, she won a contest for her essay, *"A Christmas Memory"* in the online publication, wydaily.com.

Cindy and her husband, Carl, live in Williamsburg, Virginia, where she has directed a music school for twenty-six years. They have two grown children and five grandchildren. You can visit her website: www.cindylfreeman.com to learn more.

"I was raised on a dairy farm in central New York," says Freeman. "Because I was allergic to everything from the cows to the crops that fed them, I spent a lot of time indoors while my siblings enjoyed farm life. I entertained myself by singing, playing the piano, and writing poetry, plays and stories. It never occurred to me that writing could become a career, especially since my heart's desire was to become a professional singer. Off I went to college to be a music major."

"As I devoted the next forty-five years to teaching and performing music—and raising a family--my bucket list continued to include writing. Now with retirement looming, I look forward to a fulfilling second career as a novelist." Freeman's writing appeals primarily to young women in their twenties and thirties. She enjoys the creative process of analyzing her characters' motives and making them speak and act convincingly. "I like my female protagonists to come across as strong, yet vulnerable," she says.

In her latest novel, *Unrevealed*, published by High Tide Publications, she presents Allison Harmon, a wealthy heiress, with the challenge of unraveling a well-guarded family secret. Unanswered questions have followed Allison from her childhood to the present day, haunting both her dreams and her waking thoughts. As she assumes leadership of her deceased father's billion-dollar textile industry, the strange flashbacks cause her to question her sanity.

Freeman's next project, *The Dark Room*, tackles the difficult subjects of Battered Woman Syndrome and Child Abuse. She says she hopes it will speak to women who are caught in abusive situations, giving them courage to break the cycle and hope for a better future. She is determined to give her story a happy ending.

Made in the USA
Charleston, SC
24 January 2016